W9-CBB-990

# Fear the Light

## by E. X. Ferrars

G.K.HALL &CO.
Boston, Massachusetts
1991

Published in Large Print by arrangement with
Harold Ober Associates.

G.K. Hall Large Print Book Series.

Set in 16 pt. Plantin.

**Library of Congress Cataloging-in-Publication Data**

Ferrars, E. X.
    Fear the light / E.X. Ferrars.
       p.  cm.—(G.K. Hall large print book series) (Nightingale
series)
    ISBN 0-8161-5104-0
    1. Large type books.  I. Title.
  [PR6003.R458F44   1991]
  823′.912—dc20                    90-44340

# Chapter I

"THE ROOM you always had," Mrs. Robertson said. "I know you can find it. Nowadays I don't tackle these stairs any more often than I have to."

"Of course I can find it," her nephew said. "My memory goes a long way farther back than three years. And things here don't change."

"Three years—is that really all it is?" Mrs. Robertson said. "It seems far longer. You shouldn't have stayed away so long, Charles."

"Well, now, I couldn't help it, could I?"

"Couldn't you? Anyway, you're a good boy to have come when you could."

"Suppose I say you're good to have me?"

She gave him the first real smile that he had seen on her face since he had turned his car in at the gate and she had come with her new, slow, shuffling steps to meet him at the door.

1

"Well, then, I'd have to say that you at least have changed," she said, "since I don't remember that you ever went in for so much politeness."

And that, Charles Robertson thought, sounded more like her old self. Her small dark eyes glittered humorously in her thin face. Deeply lined though it was, it had altered less than the rest of her.

"Come down when you're ready and we'll have a drink," she said and turning away from him, walked slowly and stiffly back to the fire in her sitting-room.

Charles went up the wide staircase, his hand sliding up the mahogany hand-rail. He wondered if in fact it had been foolish rather than kind to say that things here had not changed when his old aunt had changed so sadly. Yet he had meant what he had said. As soon as he had entered the house, and even before that, when from a quarter of a mile away he had first caught sight of the familiar line of the slate roof and squat chimneys showing amongst the trees, a sense of complete familiarity with everything about the place had gripped him. The budding chestnuts hanging over the low garden wall, the massed daffodils beneath them, and the lights shining in the big windows of the

2

stolid, red brick Victorian house, had taken him straight back to all the Easter holidays spent here in his boyhood. And now, going up the stairs, his feet knew the feeling of the worn old carpet under them. On the landing, without his having to pause for thought, his hand knew where to reach for the light switch.

Also, he knew which of the heavy mahogany doors to open, and when, as he pressed the switch by the door, no light came on in the room, he knew that he had simply to cross to the side of the bed and grope for the hanging switch behind it. For the lights, fitted forty years before into what had once been gas brackets, worked only if both switches were on at the same time.

That, Charles thought, was the sort of thing in this house which, it could be said for certain, would never be changed. Not, at least, as long as it belonged to Aunt Alice.

But as that thought occurred to him, he dumped his suitcase on the bed, opened it and started tossing out his belongings with the hasty, clumsy gestures of one who is trying to smother under sudden, purposeless action something that has just come into his mind. What he did not want to think about just then was that the change in his aunt might mean that the house would not belong to her much longer, that she might soon die, and that changes, many changes, would come.

Slamming the lid down on the empty suitcase, he crossed to the window and looked out.

Charles Robertson was forty. He was of medium height and slender, stooped slightly, was rather pale, had light brown hair and grey eyes. Thus there might have been nothing about him to catch the attention if it had not been for something tense, vital, almost dramatic, which showed itself even when, as now, he was standing slackly, unaware of himself, gazing out at a twilit garden. That he was not merely looking out familiarly at the stretch of lawn, the shadowy cedar, a strip of garden wall and the corner of the house next door, but was experiencing an emotion of some intensity, could have been perceived by anyone who was there to see the set of his long face with the narrow jaw and wide temples, and to notice how the way that his arms hung at his sides looked as if it were part of some expressive, though arrested gesture.

He stood there for about half a minute, then stepped back and pulled the velvet curtains together. As the rattle of the curtain-rings stopped and the heavy folds hung still, he heard footsteps overhead.

He was startled, for he had thought that there was no one in the house but his aunt and himself. Besides, there was nothing above this room but an attic in the roof. Yet someone with a light, swift tread was walking about up there, pausing, moving something, moving it again and then, after a moment, starting down the stairs. Charles went to the door of his room to see who it was.

He saw a smallish man, dressed in a stained tweed jacket, a darned pullover and flannel trousers, come down the stairs and close the door at the bottom of them. He showed some surprise at seeing Charles, muttered good evening and went on down the stairs to the hall below. Charles, following him, saw that he was carrying a bag of tools, and noticed also his big, roughened, mechanic's hands. Yet the voice in which he had spoken had seemed fairly educated.

Going to the doorway of the sitting-room, the stranger spoke to Mrs. Robertson. "I think I've settled the trouble for the present," he said, "but all the wiring in this house is so old it's practically rotted away,

5

so I don't promise you won't have any more bother. Still, if you do, just give me a ring."

He was turning to go when Mrs. Robertson, from her chair by the fire, said, "Ah, stay and have a drink with us, David. You remember my nephew, Charles, don't you? He used to come here quite often, but he lives in Scotland now and apparently that's too far away for him to come here more than very occasionally. And Charles, I'm sure you remember David Baldrey, who's come back to live at the old Baldrey farm and always helps me out when I'm in trouble. I don't know where I'd be now without him. The frozen pipes in the winter, the fuses, broken sash-cords . . . It's wonderful, isn't it, to be able to turn one's hand to anything like that *and* to know all about old pictures and china and so on?"

David Baldrey turned to Charles. His smile was diffident and singularly attractive.

"Yes, I remember you," he said, "but I don't expect you remember me. It was a long time ago that I cleared out."

"I can't honestly say I recognise you, but I remember hearing about you," Charles said.

As soon as he had heard the name, he had remembered clearly what he had heard of

David Baldrey. The son of a local farmer, he had gone into the army at eighteen, had been badly wounded, had been in a prison camp in Germany, had been decorated and for a while had been much and proudly talked about in his native village. But by degrees the talk had ceased and later, if his name had been mentioned at all, it had generally been in a tone of disparagement, as if in the end he had not turned out too well.

Yet there was something unusually appealing about him, Charles thought. His broad, rounded forehead and the clear grey of his eyes gave him a look of intelligence and candour. His diffidence was that of a man more sensitive and more complex than he wanted others to know. He had short-cropped, sandy hair, a short nose with wide nostrils, a wide mouth that looked as if it smiled easily and white, even teeth. He was almost as old as Charles, but because of the innocence in his expression, might have been many years the younger.

"Well, come in, both of you," Mrs. Robertson said, "Come in and sit down."

She seemed to have shrunk in size since Charles's last visit, and in her big, high-backed chair looked as lost as if she were a child. But at least her clothes had not changed. Charles felt fairly sure that the tweed skirt, hand-knitted jumper and string of amber beads that she was wearing, were just what she had worn throughout that visit, three years before.

"No, I won't stay now, thank you, Mrs. Robertson," David Baldrey said, still from the doorway, "or I'll miss my supper. We eat early at home now that Jean's working."

He raised a hand in a gesture of farewell that included both Charles and his aunt and went quickly away.

"Does he ever stay?" Charles asked as he came into the room.

It was big, with a high, heavily moulded ceiling. There was a great deal of furniture in the room and a great number of family photographs on the walls and tables. Worn cretonne covered the chairs.

"Sometimes," Mrs. Robertson answered. "When I'm alone. He'll sometimes stay for the evening then and never stop talking. And it's interesting talk, because he knows so much about so many different things. Only not quite enough about any one of them, poor David. Fetch the sherry, will you, Charles? Then come and sit down and tell me everything."

Charles went to the corner cupboard

where the sherry and the glasses had always been kept. He filled two glasses and brought them across the room to the fireside.

"Tell you everything about what?" he asked.

"Oh, about the last three years," Mrs. Robertson said, "and whether you still like being a business man. I hope you're at least a successful business man, Charles— though the only really successful descendants of James Robertson have been scientists like him. Insurance, however, is something quite new. I'd like to know how it's turning out."

"From the tone of your voice," Charles said as he sat down, "I don't think you expect much."

"Well, I realise you haven't got it in you to be a scientist," she said, "but I think you might have tried the stage or the church. There's a dramatic something about you that a lot of the less brilliant members of your family have and which so often seems to go bad in people if they don't have a chance to stand up and perform and be admired."

"Oh, I'm a quiet sort of character, Aunt Alice, I like peace," Charles said.

"And is insurance peaceful? And

Edinburgh—why did it have to be in Edinburgh?"

"It's where we come from, isn't it?" he said.

"How many generations ago? And it's so far away, Charles—so far that I haven't seen you for three years."

"The first two of those I was in Canada," he reminded her.

She nodded and smiled. "I'm just being querulous, my dear, because I've missed you so much. How do you like it up there?"

"I like it." He hesitated and added. "I may be getting married."

Her small eyes opened wide. "And I'd almost given up hope! Oh, Charles, I'm so delighted. Tell me about her."

"I'd be no good at that. But one day soon I'll bring her to see you."

"What's her name?"

"Sarah. Sarah Inglis. She's thirty-two and she's a teacher. And—let me think. She's got sandy hair and green eyes. She plays golf and she can't cook."

"I see what you mean about your descriptive powers," Mrs. Robertson said. "So just tell me if I'll like her."

"For certain."

"And why do you only say you *may* be

getting married? Which of you can't make up your mind?"

"Sarah can't. Because, she says, I can't. But that isn't true."

She gave a slight sigh and said, "I wish Peggie would marry, too." Peggie was her granddaughter, and since her parents' death in an air-raid, had been brought up by Mrs. Robertson and become the object of a deep, anxious love. "But she never seems to develop even the first symptoms."

"Still, she's carrying on the scientific traditions of the family very nicely," Charles said. "Isn't it pretty good at her age, and for a woman too, to have become a university lecturer?"

"Yes, of course it is, but I can't help worrying." Mrs. Robertson gave Charles an intent glance. "I suppose it was really Peggie who made you come all that long way from Edinburgh to see me."

"Why no, Aunt Alice," he lied quickly, "it wasn't."

"Ah, but you've heard from her recently, haven't you?"

"Well, I tried to see her when I was passing through London, but she was busy. We just had a talk on the telephone."

11

"And she didn't tell you to persuade me to move?"

"She did sound as if she'd feel happier about you if you did," he said. "And suppose we talk about that now. How are you? You wrote so little about your accident that I never realised how serious it was. If I'd realised . . ."

She made an impatient gesture. "It's a dull subject."

"But have you really completely recovered, or have you just been saying so, so that you'll be left in peace? And this living here alone, is it really wise?"

"Oh, I've completely recovered. That's to say . . ." Leaning back in her chair, she let her head fall wearily against the cushion behind it. That slight abandonment of the pretence of strength, that giving in to being old and ill, sent a pang of distress through Charles, and for a moment he hated himself because of his neglect of her.

"At my age, I don't suppose one ever completely recovers from anything," she said. "One can't expect ever to go back to being what one was before. And I don't suppose breaking a hip is a particularly comfortable thing to have happen to you even when you're young and active. All the same, the wretched thing's mended all right and, as you can see, I'm managing very well."

"As always, you seem to be managing wonderfully well," he said.

"It was all my own fault, of course. I was in too much of a hurry when there was ice on the roads and I simply slipped and fell."

He could imagine it. She had always been in a hurry, had always done more than seemed possible and all of it quickly, her walk a jerky little trot that had generally taken her ahead of anyone who tried to walk with her.

"All the same, why have you got to live alone?" he asked.

"Because I prefer it." The sharpness in her own voice seemed to exhilarate her. She drew herself up and reached for her glass of sherry. "And I've made myself very comfortable. I've turned the morning-room into my bedroom and I use what was once the maids' bathroom, which means that I hardly ever have to tackle the stairs. And Mrs. Harkness still comes in every morning and cleans the house and I do all my shopping by telephone. And I've friends all round me who've been good and kind. So you see, you and Peggie have nothing to worry about. Now let's talk about something else.

Tell me, what did you think of David Baldrey?"

"I liked the look of him," Charles said. "What does he do for a living?"

"The trouble is, nothing in particular," she answered. "I suppose the war had a good deal to do with it. He's really an immensely clever man and it's wonderful the amount he's taught himself without any help from anyone. But now that he's got all that knowledge locked up in his head, he hasn't the faintest idea what to do with it. He came home about eighteen months ago, but he's never even attempted to farm the land and the place has gone to rack and ruin. He does odd jobs about the place and buys and sells things and somehow keeps the wolf from the door—though most people think it's really Jean who does that, working at the White Lion. And he's a gentle, nice person . . ." She hesitated, as if she had meant to add something, then had changed her mind. "I'm sure he is," she went on, "but somehow that never seems to be enough for getting along in life, does it?"

"Who's Jean?" Charles asked.

"His sister. And in her way she's rather a misfit too, though she's got some wonderful qualities. She set out to be an actress,

14

but now she's the barmaid at the White Lion and keeps house for David. When I remember the old Baldreys, such solid, homely people, I find it all very puzzling."

"Don't any of your other neighbours bother about you—the people next door, for instance?"

But Mrs. Robertson's mind was still on David Baldrey and she did not answer the question.

"Some of David's odd bits of knowledge are really quite extraordinary," she said. "He was up in the attic one day last month, thawing out the pipe to the hotwater tank, which had frozen up in that sudden cold spell that caught us all unawares, and he got interested in some of the old lumber up there. Most of it's been there for as long as I can remember and I've always thought of it as a lot of Victorian junk that wouldn't even repay the trouble of getting rid of it. But he spotted two things which are apparently moderately valuable. One is a small portrait of James Robertson and the other is a complete run for thirty years of the Proceedings of the Royal Society, from eighteen sixty-four to ninety-four. They belonged to Frederick Robertson, of course, and I suppose have been here ever since he

15

built this house when he retired from the Chair at Cambridge. One of his daughters probably put them all away in the attic when he died—most probably Grand-aunt Christina, who, as I remember her, wasn't at all an intelligent woman. Or perhaps she was really!" She gave her little bark of a laugh. "They wouldn't have been worth much then, but now they're a nice little nest-egg for Peggie. I've really so little to leave the child that I'm thankful for anything extra. Good, clever Christina!"

Charles was not much stirred by the thought of what had been left behind by his great-grandfather, Frederick Robertson. He took a reasonable pride in his descent from that soberly distinguished, mid-Victorian scientist, but Frederick Robertson had left so much of himself behind, in the shape of writings which were now of no interest to anyone but the historian of science, and of photographs of himself with the great white beard spreading across the still greater expanse of waistcoat and gold watch chain; photographs taken at Cambridge, in London, in the Alps, in the Hebrides, surrounded by his daughters and his one son, Lancelot, or in the company of Darwin, of Huxley, of Wallace, that to hear that something more of his had been discovered in an attic made very little appeal to the imagination. Particularly this was bound to be so if he happened to have been mentioned in the same breath as his ancestor, James Robertson.

That all this time, upstairs in the attic, there had been a portrait of that other Robertson, James, the Edinburgh tailor's son, the first of his family to emerge from obscurity and who left behind a name so great that all who had borne it after him had lived in its shadow, had instantly inflamed Charles, and before his aunt had finished he had jerked forward to the edge of his chair and was trying to interrupt her.

"A portrait of old James himself! Where is it? Let me see it!"

"I'm afraid I haven't got it any more," Mrs. Robertson said.

"You haven't sold it!"

"No, but I sent it to Peggie. I thought—well, I didn't really think you'd be interested. And Peggie is the only scientist in the family now." She peered at Charles curiously, worry appearing on her face. "It isn't a good painting, Charles. David thought it might not even be contemporary. I don't think it's worth much."

17

Charles sprang to his feet, the sudden flushing of his all too expressive face revealing that he was furiously angry. It was not really that he minded Peggie's having the portrait. In his rather restless life he had not acquired much of a taste for possessions. But that he had not been told until now of the existence of the portrait, that he had not been consulted as to what should be done with it, that he had been treated—his anger mounted at the thought—as if he had sold his inheritance for a mess of pottage, all because, recognising his limitations, he had accepted a good job in an insurance company, instead of turning himself into a third-rate scientist—which was probably all, he thought ungenerously, that Peggie would ever achieve—wasn't that too much to take quietly?

"I was not," he said with bitter dignity, "thinking of the money."

"Charles, dear, I'm sorry," Mrs. Robertson said. "If I'd realised . . . But I always had the feeling you found the whole Robertson past a bit of a bore."

"Well, I'm not sure I don't," he said.

"If you want the picture, though—"

"I certainly do not," he said emphatically

and stiffly. "I don't grudge it to Peggie in the least."

"But I'm sure she wouldn't grudge it to you either, so you must talk it over when you see her. And if you can't agree between you who's to have it—"

"I've just said I don't want it," Charles said, "so there's no cause for disagreement."

"No, Charles. But that's just what Peggie will probably say too. So if you can't agree about it sensibly, I'll just send it to Professor Harlan K. Stacey, who probably deserves it much more than either of you. Now help yourself to some more sherry and I'll go and get supper." Gripping both arms of her chair with her small, bony hands, she started to pull herself very slowly to her feet.

The sight brought Charles to her side, all thought of the portrait of James Robertson driven out of his head. His arms went round her, taking her slight weight.

"Look, Aunt Alice, I'll get the supper," he said. "Just tell me what you want done and I'll do it. I'm not much of a cook but I can boil and fry fairly adequately."

She shook her head. "The doctor says it's good for me to do all I can. If I got in the habit of sitting down too much, perhaps I'd never get up again. Not that I'm going to do anything now but warm up some Irish stew. Then we can have some cheese and fruit. And I think I'll just put it all on the trolley and we'll eat here by the fire, instead of laying the table in the dining-room. I always found that room rather overpowering except when we had a real family party."

Charles let her go. He occasionally quarrelled passionately with his aunt, as he did with most of his dearest friends and relations, fortunately forgetting the quarrels even more quickly than he entered into them, but it never occurred to him to argue with Mrs. Robertson about anything that concerned herself, when it was quite clear that her mind was made up.

Helping himself to more sherry, he sat down again by the fire and with his gaze settling on the stirring flames, he thought of the question that he had asked his aunt some minutes earlier, to which she had given no reply.

It had been a very simple question. He had asked her if none of her neighbours besides the Baldreys gave her any help. For instance, he had added casually, the people next door.

Remembering this, and wondering if his

aunt's failure to answer had been as accidental as it had appeared, Charles's mouth
curved into a crooked grin of mockery at
himself.

"The people next door." That was what
he had called them, suddenly not trusting
himself, even now, to speak the name of
Deborah Heydon.

## Chapter II

"The Heydons?" Mrs. Robertson said an
hour later.

Their meal eaten, she and Charles were
sitting over their coffee. Very casually,
Charles had just repeated his question.

"Oh, yes, I still see a good deal of them,"
she said. "More than I want, sometimes.
But that's my own fault, I suppose, at least
with the children. I encouraged them too
much when they were just babies and now
that they're a wild pair of uncontrolled little
hooligans, I can hardly tell them to keep
away, even if they do trample all over my
flower-beds and shoot me dead whenever
they see me."

From her voice, Charles knew that his
aunt had no real objection to the children.

But he had been watching her keenly for any sign that she noticed his eagerness to talk about the Heydons and he had seen a shade pass over her face. He wondered if that meant that she knew how much they had had to do with his long absence.

"I used to like them both, you know," Mrs. Robertson went on. "When they first came here they seemed such a nice change from most of the people I know now. Cleverer, of course—more like it used to be in the old days when your father and your uncle were alive and all their friends used to come here. And then Ivor and Deborah were so devoted to each other and did everything together and that was so nice to see. But lately—I don't know—I find them difficult. Ivor's a rather quarrelsome man and he drinks too much, but just when I'm feeling sorriest for Deborah, she suddenly irritates me by being much too tolerant and all-forgiving. I'm sure it isn't good for him and it certainly isn't good for the children. They're developing even worse manners than he's got. I like exuberant children, but Simon and Harriet are quite out of hand and neither of their parents seems to give that a thought."

"How's Ivor's work going these days?" Charles asked.

"Well, I never could manage to read his books, you know, even when I was most charmed by him, and I'm afraid I don't even bother to try now," she said. "He uses too many words I don't know the meaning of, and his characters are all so unpleasant and never seem to say what they mean, and they quote from books I've never heard of and in odd moments commit the most horrible crimes. It's all too difficult and depressing for me. I don't think he sells any better than he used to."

There had been a time when Charles had attempted to convince his aunt that her next-door neighbour was a writer who mattered, but he had long ago given up the attempt.

"With a family to look after that must be pretty tough," he said.

"For Deborah, yes."

"But she seems quite happy?"

"Oh, my dear, how can one tell when people are happy? It's something they hardly ever know themselves. But that's just reminded me, there's a letter I want to write. It's to a man who says that the greatest happiness of his life will be meeting me,

23

and at my age, you'll grant that's quite an event. So if I write my letter quickly now, you'll be a dear and take it to the letter-box for me, won't you? I know the last post has gone, but if the letter's posted this evening, it'll go first thing in the morning."

Charles thought that the change of subject had been deliberate and felt irritated. For some time now he had been convinced that Deborah Heydon meant nothing to him, yet upstairs in his bedroom, while he had stood at the window, looking out at the two gardens, his aunt's and the Heydons', lying side by side in the dusk, a wave of the old desperation both to see Deborah and, at all costs, to keep away from her, had swept over him and terrified him. The feeling had lasted only a moment and now, in the sitting-room with Mrs. Robertson, with the drawn curtains shutting out the haunting shadows of the spring evening, he was not inclined to take his panic seriously. But still something drove him to talk about Deborah as if this were a test that he must set himself.

Thinking that he would come back to her in a moment, he asked, "Who is this happy man, Aunt Alice?"

"Professor Harlan K. Stacey," she said.

24

"He's one of those odd people who've made a hobby of the Robertson family and who know ten times as much about them as any of us. He's just arrived in England and he's hoping to make his visit a sort of pilgrimage from Robertson to Robertson, beginning with this house and me. I'd like to write and suggest all sorts of much more enjoyable things he might do with his time, but in fact, I shall, of course, say that I'll be delighted to see him next week-end, as he proposed. And naturally I'll send him on to Peggie and then to you and I hope you'll both be nice to him."

"Including handing over to him the newly discovered portrait of old James?"

"Only if you and Peggie can't decide sensibly which of you is to keep it."

"That's already decided. Peggie's keeping it."

"In any case, you'll have to show him the house where James was born. Or get him to show it to you, because I'm sure he knows every stone of it without ever having been near Edinburgh, and I don't suppose you even know where it is. And you will post my letter, won't you, Charles?"

"Of course, I will."

Gripping the arms of her chair, she began

the slow process of getting to her feet to cross the room to her writing-table.

This time Charles did not try to help her. He realised that in her deep fear of losing the independence that still made her life worth living, she truly did not want his help.

When the letter was written, she changed her mind about wanting it posted.

"I'm sure you're tired and the morning will really do just as well," she said. "If you'll put the letter on the table in the hall where we can see it, we won't forget about it."

"No, I'll take it now," Charles said. "I'd like a walk before I go to bed."

"That's like Peggie. She loves walking about alone in the dark. She's a queer girl —almost too much of a Robertson, I sometimes think. That's a great load to carry, you know, particularly for a woman." She gave him the letter. Then she suddenly lifted a hand and touched his cheek softly. "I'll say good night and go to bed now. Will you remember to lock the door when you come in?"

He promised to remember, bent and kissed her.

"And remember to bring your Sarah to see me soon."

"I will."

With the letter in his pocket, he left her and went out into the garden.

The time was a few minutes after ten o'clock, which was not what Charles was in the habit of thinking of as late, but sitting by the fire for so long had made him drowsy. Standing still for a moment, he breathed in the freshness of the cool night air. A brisk wind was stirring, carrying clusters of light cloud across the moon. It was a slender moon, a mere shaving of silver. Shining through the moving clouds, it looked as if it were having to struggle against them to force its way across the dark sky. The tree-tops shivered and made faint creaking and sighing noises.

At first Charles thought that these were the only noises of the night, but as he walked towards the gate, he caught the sound of voices coming towards him along the lane that joined the main road just opposite the gate, and even at this distance Charles recognised one of the voices. It was louder than the others, didactic and harsh. Drawing back, he waited in the deep shadow of the chestnuts beside the gate, for he had no desire just then to meet Ivor Hey-

27

don, particularly when he was on his way home after closing time at the White Lion.

Not that Charles had ever disliked Ivor. He had experienced a complex variety of feelings for him, but had never managed to dislike him. There was a naïve generosity and earnest sincerity about him which had always made it impossible. However, he was often an exhausting person to meet, because two or three drinks made him unbearably talkative, and if he saw Charles now it was not impossible that he would leave his companions, dig strong fingers into Charles's shoulder and hold him there to listen to him for half an hour.

Standing under the trees, Charles waited until Ivor and the two men who were with him, who occasionally interrupted his monologue with thick, uncomprehending laughs, had reached the corner of the lane, turned into the main road and walked a little way towards the Heydons' house and the main part of the village, which straggled along the road beyond it. Then Charles opened the gate, crossed the road and started down the lane.

About a hundred yards ahead of him, he could see the lights in the curtained upper windows of the White Lion. Those in the bar had already been put out. The building stood back from the lane with a space in front of it where cars could be parked and where, in the days before he had achieved a beer-drinking age, Charles had consumed a great deal of fizzy lemonade, sitting on a bench beside the door. Sometimes his Uncle George and sometimes his father as well had sat there with him. Charles remembered them as two quiet men, kind but distant, and so to a child rather intimidating, though certainly that had not been their intention. They had both trained as doctors, the one becoming a medical missionary in Africa, the other a professor of medicine at a London hospital. According to Charles's memory of them, they had sometimes sat there for half an hour without exchanging a word. But possibly, he thought now, his child's sense of time had exaggerated the length of their silences. They had both died a long time ago. It was nearly twenty years since his father had been buried in the village churchyard, near to his own eminent grandfather, and soon afterwards Uncle George had joined him, leaving Aunt Alice to her long widowhood.

"Good evening," a voice said suddenly out of the darkness.

Charles had still about twenty yards to go to reach the White Lion, and was opposite to the gateway of a field. Backed into this gateway was a car. If he had not been dreaming about those two old men, together in the silence that nothing could break, he would probably have noticed the car as he approached, for the night was not so dark that it was hidden, or that he could not see that the man in the driver's seat was David Baldrey.

Baldrey was just lighting a cigarette. As the match flared, the shadows behind the flame became deeper, so that his face seemed to hang above it like a mask on a wall, pale and expressionless.

"I'm waiting for Jean," Baldrey said. There was a curious childishness in the way he said it, as if he felt that he had to account for his presence there to an adult who might think it strange. "She doesn't like the walk home in the dark, so I always come and fetch her."

What struck Charles as strange was that Baldrey had chosen to wait with his car in this gateway, rather than in the car-park in front of the pub. But that was plainly Baldrey's own business.

"It's a pleasant night," Charles re-

30

marked, unable just then to think of anything else to say.

"Not bad," Baldrey agreed.

That might have been the end of the conversation. Yet Baldrey had the air of someone who wanted to talk, who was hoping not to be left immediately to his own company and his own thoughts.

Partly to meet this unexpressed demand and partly because he felt curious about the man, Charles went on, "My aunt's been telling me about your finds in her attic."

Baldrey's face brightened with his diffident, attractive smile.

"I'm afraid it must sound as if I go poking around through other people's things without having been asked," he said. "Well, I do. I can't resist it. I can't resist the sight of junk."

"Which of us can?" Charles said.

"It's a bug I've had as long as I can remember," Baldrey went on. "It's always been a sort of daydream of mine that some day I'd unearth a real treasure and have the knowledge to recognise it."

"According to my aunt, you've got the knowledge," Charles said.

"So all we need is the treasure!"

They laughed together.

"I've often wondered how one acquires that sort of knowledge," Charles went on.

"I think it's mostly a sort of instinct," Baldrey answered. "You have it or you haven't. Isn't it the same with every kind of knowledge?"

"I suppose it is."

"I mean, what's hammered into your head by other people never gets to mean much. There isn't a great deal that anyone else can teach you. But of course there's experience. That's the only thing that'll develop the instinct."

Baldrey talked quickly, with an undercurrent of excitement, as if he wanted to prove something.

"Well, you seem to have done very well with your instinct so far," Charles said.

"I say, Mrs. Robertson didn't get the idea those things I turned up are valuable, did she?" Baldrey said. "I mean, really valuable. There might be three or four hundred pounds in them, but that's all."

"What's wrong with three or four hundred pounds?"

"Well, if you put it that way . . . And tax free, eh? I suppose they'd be tax free. I mean, what about death duties?"

"You mean my aunt might have to pay

up on them because actually she inherited them from her husband?"

"And he'd have inherited them from somebody too, wouldn't he?"

"That's an unpleasant thought."

"Only perhaps it doesn't count if you go back as far as that."

"I don't know," Charles said. "I believe there's a limitation of some sort. Perhaps I ought to look into it."

"Only I don't see why anyone has to know about the things having been found," Baldrey said. "I don't suppose Mrs. Robertson's thinking of selling them, is she?"

He drew at his cigarette. As the tip glowed, it again lit up his face against the darkness and gave it that expressionless, mask-like quality.

"I'm sure she isn't," Charles said.

"Then the simplest thing would be to say nothing about it. There's no point in looking for trouble."

"But even if she found she did have to pay something on the things," Charles said, "I don't suppose it would be much. She'd still be better off than if you hadn't found them for her. I know she's delighted about it."

"Thanks—I'm glad I did then."

There was a silence, then Baldrey asked, "Are you staying long?"

"Only two or three days," Charles answered.

"That's a pity. I mean, it isn't really right for her to live alone now. Mrs. Robertson, I mean. I know Dr. Robertson thinks so, too."

It took Charles a moment to realise that the Dr. Robertson to whom Baldrey referred was Peggie, young Peggie, who, it was somehow difficult to remember, had recently acquired a Ph.D.

"My cousin's quite right, of course," Charles said. "In fact, she asked me to come here to see if I could persuade my aunt to move to London. But, as you probably know, there's no hope of making her do anything she doesn't want to."

"But she isn't as strong as she thinks," Baldrey said. "She'll fall and hurt herself again one day. She oughtn't to be alone so much."

The anxiety in his tone put Charles on the defensive. He felt as if he were being accused of something. Peggie had made him feel the same when she had written, demanding that he should visit his aunt and try to persuade her to move. And when they had spoken together for a few minutes on the telephone earlier that day, Peggie had seemed to think that where she, the beloved granddaughter, had failed, Charles ought to succeed, and that if he did not, it would be his fault, which was absurd. All the same, perhaps he had not yet tried as hard as he might.

"I'll see what I can do," he said.

"I get worried about her, you see," Baldrey said. "That's why I'm round there so much. She's a wonderful old lady and I can't stand the thought of her hobbling around alone and falling down again and not having anyone there to help her. I drop in just to make sure she's all right. There's nothing wrong with that, is there?"

"Of course not."

"You don't mind?"

"No, of course not."

There was another silence. Baldrey gave him one of the looks which suggested that he expected, or at least hoped, that Charles would say something more, but after a short hesitation Charles only said good night and went on his way to post his aunt's letter.

The letter-box was some distance beyond the White Lion, a building of grey stone with a roof of silvery, moss-grown tiles. The lion on the inn sign had always been less white than grey and so sad and furtive looking that it might just have been caught out in some minor and despicable sin. But now, as Charles passed by and saw the sign in the faint moonlight, it seemed to him that all the old sorrow had disappeared behind a cheerfully ferocious grin and that the grey pallor of the despondent beast had become a white so clean and bright that it almost shone. There was no doubt about it, the sign had been repainted.

After that, it was not much of a surprise that other small landmarks along the lane had changed. A little way beyond the inn there was a bus stop where he could not remember that there had been one before. Farther on, at the point where the lane curved to the right round the edge of a small reedy pond, a white railing had been erected for safety along the edge of the road. Thirty yards or so beyond the pond, a cottage which Charles remembered as almost a ruin, roofed with disintegrated thatch, which was full of birds' nests, had now a tiled roof and electric light shining through rose-pink curtains.

The letter-box was only a little way beyond the cottage. It was on the opposite side of the road, at a corner where the lane was joined by another. When Charles had posted the letter to Professor Harlan K. Stacey, he felt inclined to return to the house by this second lane, which curved back to the main road past the Baldrey farmhouse. But to do so would take him far longer than to return by the way that he had come and he thought that possibly his aunt might start wondering what had become of him. Turning, he started back towards the White Lion.

As he reached the bend in the lane beside the pond, a beam of powerful headlights swept the road from behind him. His own shadow leapt ahead of him. Moving to one side, he waited beside the new white railings to let a double-decker bus pass by. Its lights gave him a glimpse of Baldrey's car, still in the gateway beyond the pub, then of his aunt's house facing him at the end of the lane. Then the bus swung round the corner towards the village and disappeared and the lane seemed suddenly darker than it had before. Reaching the car, Charles saw again the gleam of a cigarette inside it and the blur of a face above the cigarette. But this time, only raising a hand and seeing the gesture returned, he went straight on. A minute or two later, he let himself into the house.

In the doorway he stood still, unbelieving, the breath shocked out of him.

The light, which was on as he had left it, showed him his aunt lying in a heap halfway up the stairs. Her head was nearer to him than her feet, her white hair straggled over the carpet and her eyes were staring.

# Chapter III

AT THAT moment the telephone started to ring.

It did not even occur to Charles to answer it. The sound, which seemed to continue endlessly in the deadly silence of the house, was like a knife, cutting its way into his brain. It paralysed him until it stopped.

When at last it did, he managed to draw a long breath and to take a few uncertain steps forward. Then all at once his muscles came under his control again and he took the stairs three at a time.

Kneeling beside Mrs. Robertson, he put a hand inside the quilted dressing-gown that she was wearing to feel for the heart-beat that could not be there. This was a ritual that had to be performed. He was still too shocked for feeling and in such moments only ritual makes sense.

He was asking himself frantically what she had been doing on the stairs. She had told him that she avoided them, living entirely on the ground floor. So what had made her toil up them unsteadily and probably suffering pain as she went, to lose her balance, slip and fall?

David Baldrey's words sang in his ears. "She'll fall and hurt herself again one day . . . She oughtn't to be alone so much . . ."

Had she thought suddenly that while Charles was gone she would go up to his room to make sure that all was well there, that it had been made comfortable and welcoming for him?

The thought started him trembling, as if this made him to blame for her death.

His next thought was to gather her up in his arms, carry her to her room, lay her on her bed and cover her. For there was something brutally grotesque about the way that she was lying, head downwards, with her thin white hair straggling loosely over the edge of a stair.

But even as his arms went out to her, he checked the gesture. You weren't supposed

39

to move them, were you? You weren't supposed to touch anything.

His heart drummed harder as he realised that he had already taken in something which probably made it particularly important that she should not be moved. This was that on the landing above, the door at the bottom of the attic staircase was standing wide open.

Charles was not in a state to think clearly about this, yet he did know what it was that he had to do immediately. He had to telephone the police. And, of course, a doctor, although there was nothing that a doctor could do for Mrs. Robertson. But there was a sort of decency, a propriety, about having one to stand by her when the police came to peer at her, photograph her and stand around and ask their questions about her.

But when Charles tried to remember the name of the doctor in the village, the only one that came to his mind was that of a man who had seen him through one or two childish illnesses and who had retired years ago. Mrs. Robertson had never been a woman whose illnesses and doctors had been prominent in her conversation and though someone local must have attended her after her accident, Charles did not think that he had heard his name.

So after all there was nothing to be done but call the police and leave the matter to them.

On his way to the telephone, however, he thought that David Baldrey would know the name of the village doctor. Going to the door, Charles pulled it open, went out on to the doorstep, gave a shout and waved. The shout sounded shockingly loud to him and he knew that his figure must be visible against the light streaming out of the door, but nothing happened. Then the shifting mist of cloud suddenly left the moon clear and its light grew bright enough for him to see that Baldrey's car was no longer in the lane.

Turning back into the house, Charles closed the door and went to the telephone. Just as his hand went out to it, it started to ring again.

He snatched it up and said hoarsely, "Hallo!"

A man's voice said, "I've a telegram for Mrs. Alice Robertson."

In his relief that this was not some friend of his aunt's ringing up, Charles found himself able to speak more naturally.

"She—she isn't here," he said. "But I'll take it."

The voice went on, "It's signed 'Harlan K. Stacey'—H for Harry, A for Arthur, R for Robert—"

"All right, all right," Charles said, "I've got that."

"The message is, 'Hope to call on you to-morrow Saturday as proposed looking forward eagerly to meeting.'"

"To-morrow!" Charles said wildly.

"I'll repeat it. 'Hope to call on you to-morrow Saturday as proposed looking forward eagerly to meeting.' Do you want a copy of this?"

"No, thank you . . . Yes!"

But even as Charles changed his mind, thinking that anything that happened that evening might be of the greatest importance and that some policeman might decide that he wanted a copy of the telegram, the line went dead.

Well, if anyone wanted a copy, Charles thought, it could always be got.

But why was Professor Stacey arriving to-morrow, instead of in a week's time, as Mrs. Robertson had believed?

Putting down the telephone, Charles waited a moment, then picked it up again

42

and asked the operator for the police station. In reply to the information that Charles gave to the constable who answered, he was told that the police would be round immediately and to wait where he was.

At first he took this order so literally that he stayed in the sitting-room near to the telephone, half expecting it to ring again, even half hoping that it would, because the sound would be like company in the silent house. Straining his ears for the arrival of the police, he began after a minute or two to feel that since there had not yet been any screech of tyres on the road, any pounding on the door, some blunder must have been made and the police gone roaring off to the wrong place. And if there was any risk of that having happened, oughtn't he to ring up again to make sure? His hand started to go out to the telephone. But it was then that he thought again of the attic door.

He was quite certain that when David Baldrey came down from the attic, he had closed that door.

Going out into the hall, nerving himself to pass his aunt's body, Charles took the stairs at a rush, turned on the light on the landing, then climbed the flight up to the attic more slowly. In the darkness at the top he hesitated, thinking that he ought not to touch the light switch, in case whoever had been up there had left his fingerprints upon it. Instead, he fumbled in his pocket for his cigarette lighter and flicked it on.

Its small flame showed him low rafters, the bulky shapes of a tank and water pipes, of chests and trunks, and between everything shadows. Shadows so deep that they might have had substance. One of the trunks was open, with a pile of books on the rough floor beside it. Charles had taken a step towards it when the telephone rang again.

He felt an instant conviction that this time it was Sarah, ringing up from Edinburgh. He had not been expecting her to ring him up, had no reason for believing that it was she, yet as he raced down the stairs he felt her presence as clearly as if she had called up to him from the door. He reached the telephone before it had stopped ringing and said breathlessly, "Hallo!"

The instrument crackled in his ear but no one spoke.

"Hallo, hallo!" he said more loudly. "Who's there?"

Again there was only silence. But just as he was about to slam the telephone down, he heard an abrupt laugh and the loud, harsh voice of Ivor Heydon said, "Of course—it's you, Charles. I'd forgotten you were going to be around. I hope I didn't disturb you. I was just ringing up to see if anything's wrong, but hearing a man's voice, I thought I'd got a wrong number."

Ivor's voice was of the kind that booms on the telephone and can be heard all over the room. Sharply disappointed that this was not Sarah, and almost angry with her for having led him to make such a foolish mistake as to be certain that it would be, Charles removed the receiver an inch or two from his ear and asked, "Why did you think something was wrong, Ivor?"

"I saw lights upstairs and knew of course that Mrs. Robertson didn't go up if she could help it," Ivor answered. "Stupid of me. Sorry. Well, it's nice to know you're here, Charles. When you've time, come over and have a drink. Deborah will be glad to see you."

"Hold on, Ivor! Those lights upstairs— when did you see them?"

"Why, just now, just before I rang up."

"The landing light?"

"Yes, I suppose that's what it was."

"Oh . . . Yes, that must have been when

45

I turned it on. You didn't see anything a bit earlier, did you?"

There was a pause, then Ivor said, "Look, Charles, something *is* wrong, isn't it?"

"Well, as a matter of fact . . ." Charles was uncertain what he ought to say before the police arrived, but then, without his really having made up his mind on this point, words came in a rush. "Yes, something's wrong. Aunt Alice is dead. I went out to post a letter for her and came back and found her. She's lying half-way up the stairs. I thought at first she'd fallen, but now—well, I've called the police. They ought to be here at any minute."

So softly that Charles only just heard the words, Ivor muttered, "Good God!" After it Charles heard the hiss of his sharply drawn breath.

"I take it you didn't see anything or hear anything," Charles said.

As he spoke, he heard on the telephone another voice, too faint for him to catch any words. Someone in the other house was speaking to Ivor.

He gave some muffled answer, then in a voice that boomed as loudly as it had at first, he spoke again. "No, I saw nothing and I heard nothing. I only got in a few minutes ago and I wouldn't even have seen the lights go on if I hadn't been on my way upstairs and seen them through the staircase window, which happens not to have a curtain . . . What? Oh, all right." This was again to the person who was in the room with him. "Hold on a minute, Charles. Deborah wants to speak to you."

But although there had been no shriek of tyres in the road, or pounding of knuckles on the front door, which, to even a moderate film-goer like Charles, seemed the natural way for the police to arrive on the scene of a major crime, he knew from the sound of quiet voices in the garden that in fact they had come.

"Not now, the police have just got here," he said. "I'll ring up later."

When he opened the front door, he saw several men standing outside in the dark garden. The first to come into the house was a big, solidly built man who introduced himself as Detective-Inspector Long. He had sleek fair hair smoothed back from a big, blunt-featured face, a tight mouth and small grey eyes in which, as he turned after a moment from gazing up at the dead body of Alice Robertson to look at Charles, there was no shock, no anger, no distress, but only a cold knowingness. Before this, Charles found himself thinking, it would be the easiest thing in the world to panic blindly.

This made him resentful of Inspector Long before they had exchanged more than the first terse words of greeting. And resentment, or any form of anger, always brought out the histrionic streak in Charles. It made him dramatise himself in a way which, as he realised even while he was doing it, was hardly likely to make a good impression on the police. In answer to the inspector's quite sympathetically voiced inquiry as to where he had been when Mrs. Robertson had met her death, Charles answered in a more distracted way than was necessary. "I was out—out for a short walk, posting a letter. She asked me to post the letter. Then she said she'd missed the post anyway, the letter could wait till the morning. But I said I'd like a walk. And so she was killed, because if I hadn't gone out then, it wouldn't have happened. I mean, she wouldn't have been alone. So I feel—I feel—" He could not go on.

Inspector Long merely nodded slightly, which made Charles feel foolish.

48

"It doesn't seem to have taken you long, Mr. Robertson, to make up your mind that this wasn't an ordinary accident," Long said.

"No."

"Yet it's one of the most ordinary accidents there is, you know—an old lady falling downstairs."

"But what was she doing on the stairs? She told me herself she didn't go up them. And then there's the door to the attic."

"What about the door to the attic?"

"I know it was shut earlier in the evening, but now it's open."

Long turned his head, looking up towards the landing above.

"When was it shut?" he asked.

"When Baldrey came down."

"Baldrey?" Long said quickly. "When was he here?"

Though he was hardly aware of it at the time, it fixed itself in Charles's mind at that moment that the name of Baldrey was known to the police. Not that that meant anything in a village.

"When I arrived," Charles answered. "About six o'clock. He'd been up in the attic doing some repairs to the electrical wiring up there and I saw him come down and shut the door."

"I see. Yes. But why shouldn't it have been Mrs. Robertson herself who opened the attic door?"

"I told you, she didn't go upstairs. She was pretty lame, because of a fall she had last year."

"Yet something took her upstairs to-night."

"Yes, I know. What I mean is, it must have been something exceptional."

"Like thinking she heard someone up there when she thought she was alone in the house?"

"Yes."

"Is that really the sort of thing she'd have done?" Long asked incredulously. "A lame old lady—she'd have gone upstairs to look for a burglar?"

Charles saw that he had not made much impression on the inspector.

"Yes," he said deliberately. "It is. It is just the sort of thing she would have done."

"I see. Well, we must talk more about this presently. If you don't mind now. . . ."

Charles found himself eased into the sitting-room and left there to himself, while things from which on the whole he was grateful to be excluded went forward in the hall and on the stairs.

The room felt cold, for the fire had almost died. Besides that, there was another chill in it, or it might have been in Charles himself, a chill that he had never felt before. He crossed to the fireplace and was stirring the ashes with the poker when the door opened and Ivor Heydon came in.

He was a big man, broad-shouldered and heavy, with a short, thick neck and long, thick arms and legs. His face was pouchy and florid, with a thinning fuzz of dark brown hair above it and a short nose, shaped like the flattened, predatory beak of a bullfinch. His black eyes were bright and restless. They were observant and intelligent, yet their animation, it had always seemed to Charles, like his swift, loud speech, acted as a shield between him and the world around him, rather than as a help to communication with it. Their unrevealing stare, made slightly glassy now, Charles thought, by drink, moved here and there about the room, resting only for an instant on Charles's face.

"This is a fearful thing, Charles," he said excitedly. "You know, I hardly believed I'd heard you properly just now when you said

51

it was murder. Well, you didn't exactly say that, but it was what you meant, wasn't it? I thought it was hysteria and so did Deborah. After all, who'd think of murdering Mrs. Robertson? Why? What for? And I've just been having a word with one of those fellows out there, a man with a great blank face that looks as if it might have been made by a kid playing with Plasticine. Heaven help us if that's the sort of man who's put in charge when these things happen. Explains the crime wave, doesn't it? If there *is* a crime wave and it isn't just that violence gets a lot more publicity than it used to. I'm against that myself. I don't say the printed word will ever sow the seed of murder in a mind that isn't already fertile soil for the idea. It won't. Words mean very little to most people. But you can liken them to the shower that makes the damned seed grow . . ."

Either something in Charles's face, or the sound of his own shower of words falling on obviously barren ground, suddenly silenced Ivor. He thrust a hand through his scanty hair, frowned helplessly and muttered, "I'm damned sorry about it. Can't say how sorry."

As Charles, deciding that the fire was past

saving, withdrew from it and dropped wearily into a chair, Ivor went to stand with his back to the fireplace.

"It must have been a prowler," Ivor said. "A tramp. If it really was a murder and not an accident. Not that I can believe that. And not that we get many tramps along this way. They're a vanishing breed. Have you realised that? The honest to goodness tramp that one used to see has practically disappeared. Our children won't know what the word means. But I suppose someone might have got the word that she was an old woman, living all alone, and come in to see what he could pick up."

"And gone straight up to the attic?"

Ivor gave him one of his swift, worried glances, then looked at a corner of the ceiling.

"I don't understand," he said.

"As it looks to me," Charles said, "Aunt Alice heard something upstairs. She knew I'd gone out, so she knew it couldn't be me. If she'd been a different person, she'd have waited for me to get back, but she was always completely fearless, so she simply started upstairs on her own to investigate."

"And met her murderer?"

"Yes."

"Who gave her a push?"

"Yes."

"Why shouldn't she simply have slipped and fallen?"

All over again, Charles explained about the open door of the attic.

When he finished, Ivor gave a shake of his head. "That doesn't make particularly good sense to me. As you said yourself, why should a prowler go straight up to the attic? He'd much more likely go to the kitchen after food, or look for jewellery in Mrs. Robertson's bedroom, or the silver in the dining-room. I should think the probability is you were wrong and Baldrey didn't shut the door properly when he came down from the attic and the wind blew it open."

"It could be a mistake to stick too hard to the idea of a prowler," Charles said.

"It might be a mistake to think too hard at all," Ivor said. "Leave that to the man with the Plasticine face. It's his job and he's paid for it and you'll get no thanks if you try to do it for him. Come over and have a drink, Charles. Come to think of it, you'd better come and stay the night. The spare room's probably a mess, with the kids' things scattered all over it, but it'll be better than sleeping here."

"Thanks, Ivor, it's good of you, but I think I'd better sleep here," Charles answered. "I'd like to come over for the drink, but I don't know when I could manage it. I've been told to wait here till they're ready for me."

"Come over when you can, then. We'll probably be up pretty late. This isn't the sort of thing that makes one look forward to a good night's rest. I have as many nightmares as I can cope with in the ordinary course of events, and I don't like the idea of what'll get going in my head if I fall asleep. D'you get nightmares, Charles? I mean the sort of dream from which you wake up sick with terror, though when you go over what happened in the dream, you can't see what was frightening about it. Yet you may be haunted by it all day. And sleeping pills only make it worse and even drink doesn't help much, though it sometimes makes you forget what's ahead. I've had nightmares all my life, sometimes less, sometimes more . . ." He stopped, as if it had just occurred to him that Charles might have other things on his mind than someone else's bad dreams. "Well, come over whenever you want to," Ivor said and went to the door. Then, as he reached it, he paused.

"By the way, where's Peggie. Does she know about—this?"

"Not yet," Charles said.

"Hadn't you better tell her?"

"Yes," Charles agreed. "I'll do it now."

He felt in his pocket for the note-book in which he had recorded the address of Peggie's recently acquired flat in Highgate and her telephone number, and as Ivor went out, he dialled the operator and gave the London number.

There was a short delay, then Charles heard the telephone begin to ring in Peggie's flat. He stood there, holding it as it rang and rang, almost relieved that there was no answer. A girl of Peggie's age, he thought, can change very much in three years. In the short conversation that he had had with her on the telephone that morning, her voice had sounded like that of a different person from the girl whom he remembered. It had become cool, clipped and deliberate, with all the old impulsiveness either eradicated or controlled. He felt now as if it were a stranger to whom he would have to give the news of her grandmother's death.

Inspector Long, coming in just then, accompanied by a pink-faced sergeant said, "Trying to get Dr. Robertson? They've had a go already from the police station, but she seems not to be at home."

There was nothing in his voice to suggest that the fact that Peggie was not at home seemed to him to have any sinister importance, yet suddenly Charles felt a thumping of the heart and the same chill as he had felt when he had come into this room.

So Peggie was a suspect. And so, of course, was he. And there would be others. Perhaps Ivor. Perhaps Deborah. And heaven knew who else.

This thought made Charles straighten his slightly stooping shoulders and prepare to be the man who defends his friends to the last.

## Chapter IV

IT WAS not required of him, for Long's questions were few and, as it seemed to Charles, purely formal.

At just what time, Long wanted to know, had Charles left the house to post Mrs. Robertson's letter to Professor Harlan K. Stacey? Had Charles set off down the lane straight away, or had he lingered first in the garden? How long had he stood talking to

David Baldrey? Had Baldrey's car still been there when Charles returned? When Charles said that it had, Long seemed to lose interest in the whole matter, as if Baldrey were the only person whom it was worth suspecting.

A feeling of acute irritation began to develop in Charles and he decided that Ivor had been right, the man was stupid. Also Ivor had somehow found the right word when he had said that Long's face, with its look of having been clumsily prodded into shape by unskilful fingers, might have been modelled in Plasticine. It was immature—unsubtle. Not that one ought ever to go too much by the face. Charles decided not to be prejudiced.

But as he became convinced that he had entirely failed to impress Long with his belief that Mrs. Robertson's death had not been an accident, Charles felt something more violent than irritation begin to develop. To anyone who did not know him well, this would not have been apparent, for he became even quieter than before and chose his words with more care. Against what felt like Long's actual resistance to being given information that he did not want, Charles insisted on telling him about Baldrey's finds in the attic. There was a portrait of James Robertson, Charles said, and there were some old copies of the Proceedings of the Royal Society, which, he had been given to understand, might have a modest value. And might it not be possible, he suggested, that someone had heard a rumour of these finds, no doubt highly exaggerated, and come to rob the attic?

Long gave a brief nod of his head.

"But then anything's possible," he said. "There's nothing too small and almost nothing too big, that I've ever heard of, to seem a perfectly good motive for murder to someone or other."

"You mean you never worry much about motive?" Charles asked.

"Oh, no, I don't mean that at all," Long said. "But you wouldn't begin there, would you? Not while you're still quite uncertain whether that door at the bottom of the attic stairs was really shut when you went out, as you yourself believe, or whether perhaps it mightn't have been blown open by the wind. It's quite a windy night, and when you opened the front door to go out and post the letter, there'd have been a strong draught through the house."

"Have you made an experiment on those

lines? Does the door upstairs come open by itself when you open the front door?"

"If it isn't securely latched, it does."

"So really you've already decided that my aunt wasn't murdered."

"It isn't for me to decide that," Long said. "That'll be decided at the inquest."

"In your own mind, however . . ." But Charles did not go on. The man had a perfect right not to tell him what was in his own mind. He said instead, "Is there nothing at all you can do to determine how the door came to be open?"

"We're checking fingerprints, naturally," Long said. "If there are any on the door, or the light switches, or the banisters, which it's difficult to account for, that will be an important piece of evidence."

But he did not expect to find any such fingerprints, Charles could see that. And though Long had not said so, it seemed more than probable that he did not really believe Charles that the door to the attic stairs had ever been closed. If Baldrey should say that he had not closed it, Long would believe him.

Charles felt himself begin to tremble inwardly with the force of his repressed anger. For fear that the trembling should show, he began to walk quickly up and down the room, gesticulating with one hand, keeping the other clenched in a pocket. He repeated to Long that Mrs. Robertson would never have started up the stairs unless she had had some quite exceptional reason. And mightn't it at least be a good idea, he suggested, to call on Dr. Robertson, or on Mrs. Harkness, who had worked for years in this house, to find out, if possible, if anything was in fact missing from the attic? Because, if something were missing, that would be significant, wouldn't it?

"Naturally we shall do that," Long answered, with a flatness in his voice which implied boredom. "We shall do that in the morning."

With that, the interview closed. Quietly, as they had arrived, the police went away, taking with them the body of Alice Robertson, to lay it, as Charles unhappily visualised, on some slab in an ugly mortuary, and leaving Charles to the surprising realisation that he would have felt less furious and less scared if they had suspected him or one of his friends of his aunt's murder, rather than thus refusing to suspect anyone at all.

That he felt the cold sense of fear that he did at his failure to convince them of what he himself believed was deeply bewildering. Why should he suddenly be so afraid? Was it at the thought of a murderer walking securely among future victims? Or was it at the thought of the responsibility that had fallen on to his own shoulders? He had had experience of responsibility in his work and was not usually afraid of it. But that was a different kind of responsibility, one that stimulated him, whereas this only appalled him.

All at once he could not bear the room any longer and went out into the garden. In the house next door there were still lights downstairs, which meant, he supposed, that Ivor and Deborah had not yet gone to bed. Charles looked towards the house uncertainly. He wanted company badly but despised himself for this. As he hesitated, a gust snatched the door out of his hand and slammed it behind him. The wind tore at the tree-tops, filling the air with restless noise. The night had grown colder and the clouds had massed darkly together, hiding the moon.

Charles walked slowly towards the gate. He supposed that he had loved his aunt almost as much as he had ever loved anyone until he had met Sarah Inglis. He didn't really count Deborah. That had been a queer, quiet madness of the spirit in which he might have lost himself for ever if he had not had the strength of mind to tear himself away, but which now seemed merely to have been spun out of fantasy and hardly to have been a matter of flesh and blood. His love for the old woman who had died that night had had foundations and substance. Yet he had taken it for granted and had neglected her. When she had been ill, he had stayed away from her. Without even taking her into his confidence, telling her why he stayed away, he had let the last three years of her life go by without once coming to see her. He had written only a few times and had sent her Christmas cards.

Such thoughts were bad company and Charles started to hurry.

The Heydons' door was opened to him by Deborah. Standing with the light behind her, she looked at him, motionless. Her hair had a shining fairness and with the light gleaming through it, made a bright frame for her small shadowed face. She was a slender woman of about the same height as Charles. Because of her long neck, her slightly sloping shoulders, her small waist and the delicacy of her hands and feet, she always had a look of fragility, but when she moved some of this disappeared, for her gestures were swift and vital.

Both her hands came out to Charles swiftly.

As he took them, he said, "May I come in for a little? I know it's very late."

"We've been hoping you'd come," she said, drew him inside and shut the door. "Ivor's told me about Mrs. Robertson, of course. It's awful. It's—oh, it's awful." As always, her voice had a blurred softness, the words running hastily and indistinctly into one another.

This house was much older than the one next door and the ceiling of the little hall was so low that it cleared their heads by only a few inches. The floor was stone-paved and there were dark beams in the walls. An oak chest stood against one wall, a bookcase against another. There were flowers in a copper bowl on the chest. Everything was just as it had been when Charles had last been there, including the fact that the flowers were rather withered, that the copper bowl was tarnished, that a cobweb clung to the light and that a smell of garlic and some strong cheese was heavy on the air.

Deborah had always been a helplessly untidy woman, often distracted by her own lack of competence, capable only at cooking and there always anxious for praise. Yet Charles had always felt that essentially she was the most serene person whom he had ever known. In her intense and confident devotion to Ivor, which had made Charles's passion for her scarcely a problem to her, she had found all that she needed to live at peace with herself.

Standing close to Charles and looking at him intently, she said, "Ivor says you say it wasn't an accident. But he says it isn't possible. *I* don't think it's possible either. Poor Charles—you must have had a most terrible shock, but it isn't possible, you know. I mean . . ." Her blurred voice hesitated. "Is it?" she added.

"The police don't seem to think it is," Charles answered.

The sight of Deborah disturbed him, but not in a way that he had expected. In the moment of meeting he had thought that there had been as little change in her as in her surroundings. The blouse that looked as if it had been worn for a week, the ladder in one of her stockings, the old velvet bedroom slippers with a toe coming through

65

the end of one of them, might have been what she had been wearing when he had seen her last. Her pink lipstick was almost as smudged as a smear of strawberry jam. Her own beauty was something which she either accepted so casually, or else under-rated so grievously that she could hardly ever be persuaded to pay any attention to her appearance. Yet she had always seemed contented with it, unselfconscious and full of a quiet, infectious, almost childish gaiety, and her spontaneity had been as refreshing as a swift-flowing stream. But there was no contentment, no serenity now in her face. Small blotches of red stood out harshly on her cheekbones. Her mouth had tightened and fine lines had begun to etch themselves at its corners. Her blue eyes, which had always had a soft, unfocused gaze, mainly because she was short-sighted and would not wear glasses, had the nervous glitter of anxiety and had blue-black circles round them.

This went to Charles's heart in a way for which he was wholly unprepared and for the first time since he had fallen in love with Ivor's wife, he furiously and bitterly hated Ivor. For who but Ivor could have wrought the change? Who but Ivor had ever mattered enough to Deborah to work any change in her?

She nodded with a kind of eagerness when Charles said that the police did not think that Mrs. Robertson had been murdered and said, "Oh, no, they couldn't. Because it couldn't be, could it? I mean to say, *why* . . . ? And *who*, of course. Oh, no. But I'm so glad to see you, Charles, though I wish it hadn't been like this. Only you know I wish that. I'm being stupid. Come in and have a drink. You look as if you need one."

With a hand on his arm, she drew him into the sitting-room.

It was a big, untidy room with some good furniture in it, which, unfortunately, had never been protected from the onslaughts of the Heydon children. There were books in bookshelves and on the floor. There were toys in the chairs. There were a fishing-rod, a walking-stick and a rook-rifle leaning together in a corner. There was an overflowing work-basket on a window-seat.

Ivor was in a chair by the fire. He had a glass of whisky in his hand. His face was flushed. Turning his head, he gave Charles a long, sullen, silent stare, rose, poured some whisky into a glass, handed it to

Charles, went back to his chair and resumed his frowning concentration on the fire.

"I tried to get hold of Peggie," Charles said. "She wasn't in."

It did not seem to occur to Ivor that this required an answer. Then abruptly he turned his head again and said, "So she still doesn't know."

"No."

"I think she ought to know." It was said as if Charles had disputed the point.

"So do I," Charles said, "and I was going to say, if you've no objection, I'll try telephoning her again from here. She's probably got home by now."

"Of course, go ahead," Deborah said. She lit a cigarette, sat down in a low chair and drew her feet up under her. "The telephone's next door in Ivor's study."

Ivor came suddenly to his feet. "Haven't I told you, I don't like people mucking about in my room? I'll telephone her myself."

He went with long, not quite steady steps to the door.

Charles began, "Don't you think I'd better . . . ?"

The look on Deborah's face stopped him.

When the door had closed behind Ivor, she drew a long, shuddering breath.

"Thank you, Charles," she said. "If you'd tried to stop him we'd have had a scene. He's terribly upset about Mrs. Robertson, and he's been drinking ever since he got back. It doesn't help, yet it's what he always does when he's upset. You can't stop him."

"It isn't only when he's upset, is it?" Charles said.

"It's only then that it's serious. Not that it's really serious even then, but you know what I mean."

Charles thought that he did. He thought that Ivor's drinking was probably fairly serious all the time, but that Deborah either hid this from herself or hoped that she could hide it from others.

"But what about Peggie?" he said uneasily. "He isn't in a state to break the news particularly gently."

"Don't worry about that. He can always pull himself together when he wants to. Now sit down and have your drink in peace, Charles. You've had enough to take this evening."

Charles remained standing. "Why does

he do it?" he asked. "What's gone wrong with him?"

"Oh, he's always done it," she said.

"I don't remember it."

"You just didn't notice."

"Didn't I? But I used to watch him like a cat, Deborah. I used to watch him and brood over him and wonder what you saw in him. If he'd had such an obvious defect, it would have delighted me."

"Oh no, you aren't so malicious." A little smile flickered across her tired, anxious face. "Of course, he's at a difficult age. It's a thing, I suppose, that happens to everyone, but it's harder for some than for others. I mean, facing the fact that perhaps you aren't ever going to be a real success—if you aren't, I mean. If you've always believed in your own talents and always taken for granted when you were young that you were bound to end up something important, and then getting to the sort of age when you begin to realise that isn't ever going to happen—that's a terribly difficult thing to face."

"And Ivor's having to face it?"

"Well, actually, I suppose, he isn't facing it—and that's the trouble."

"Then is his work going really badly?"

70

"If you mean financially, it's just about the same as usual. Of course, prices keep going up, but still, we can keep body and soul together. Luckily, we haven't awfully expensive tastes. But whether or not he's satisfied with his own work—oh, I don't know. I think myself he works at it much too hard and worries too much. In his way he's got a terrific sense of responsibility, and he worries so about us all, particularly the children."

"While you worry about him," Charles said.

"But then, I always have. It's my life-work, worrying about Ivor. I don't know where I'd be without it."

She looked into his eyes as she said it. Charles realised that she had just deliberately let him know, in case the matter should have retained any importance in his mind, that her husband still meant as much to her as he always had.

Far from regretting this, Charles found that there was a curious reassurance, in the midst of the night's horror, in finding that certain things in certain people did not change. There was a rightness, a grace, in Deborah's continuing love for Ivor by which Charles was in a mood just then to be deeply moved.

"I suppose Peggie will come down here to-morrow," he said. "Does she come down here much?"

Deborah gave a start, as if her thoughts had gone far away. It occurred to Charles that she was listening for Ivor.

"Oh, she comes from time to time," she said. "Have you seen her recently?"

"Not since I went to Canada."

"She's altered a great deal. She's become very much . . ." She paused, frowned and seemed unable to find the word she wanted.

"Very much the career-woman, one of the scientist Robertsons?" Charles suggested.

"Well, perhaps she has, though that isn't what I meant. I don't know how to put it. But you'll see for yourself." As if waiting for Ivor to return had all at once become a strain that was difficult to bear, she got up, went to the door and stood waiting there.

It was a minute or two before he came back to the sitting-room. The tension in Deborah as she waited made it almost impossible for Charles to talk to her. He sipped his whisky and decided that as soon as he had heard from Ivor whether or not he had found Peggie at home, he would say good night and go.

Ivor, reappearing, saw that Charles's glass was nearly empty and tried to refill it.

"No, thanks," Charles said. "I'd better get back now. I'm really awfully tired."

"And you're going to bed in that house? And you think you're going to sleep? You can't have a nerve in your body." Ivor was refilling his own glass. "I shan't sleep. Might as well not go to bed. Might as well stay up and work. D'you know something, Charles?—work's a wonderful way of keeping the nightmares at bay. Almost the only one. Everything else makes them worse in the end."

Charles was waiting for him to say something about Peggie, but it did not seem to occur to Ivor that there was any need to do so. Going back to his chair by the fire, he dropped into it and again fixed his moody gaze on the embers.

"Well?" Deborah said in a high, sharp voice that was quite unlike her normal way of speaking. "What's Peggie going to do?"

"Do?" Ivor said vaguely.

"Is she coming down here to-morrow?" She was watching him with desperate intentness, as if every small movement that he made were important to her.

"I'm not sure what she said. But she was in all right—that's the main thing, isn't it? Said she'd been in all the evening, as a matter of fact. Heard the telephone go some time ago, but was in her bath, couldn't be bothered to answer it. So that's all right. Quite all right." Ivor turned his head to look up at Charles. "Nothing to worry about, Charles. I knew there wasn't all along, but it's best to make sure, isn't it?"

Charles went rigid. It seemed to him an obscenity to hear thoughts which had become almost conscious in his own mind, but which he had been pushing back into the shadows, spoken so casually in that morose, slurred voice.

He might have started to say this if he had not felt Deborah's hand on his arm, pushing him towards the door.

She went with him to the gate. She walked to it in a quick, purposeful way, as if she intended, once she was out of earshot of Ivor, to say something. Yet when she reached the gate, she seemed to change her mind, only said good night quickly and turned to go.

"Deborah, wait a moment," Charles said.

"What did Ivor mean by that? He says Aunt Alice's death was an accident, yet he suspected Peggie of murdering her."

"He didn't. He didn't mean anything," Deborah said. "You saw the state he's in."

"Yes, but he knew what he was saying."

She pressed her hands together, looking into Charles's face with a peculiar look of indecision.

"You don't really and truly believe it was murder, do you, Charles?" she said.

"Yes, I do, Deborah."

"Just because a door was open that you think was shut?"

"I know it was shut."

She gave her head a little shake. "It's so awfully easy to be wrong about things like that. Why do you *want* it to be murder?"

"Good God, I don't!"

"Are you sure?"

He returned her gaze with bewilderment. "Of course, I don't."

Her hands fluttered apart, then came tightly together again. "Tell me something, then. Was Mrs. Robertson—? Did Mrs. Robertson—? No, I can't say it. Anyway, it isn't important. Good night, Charles."

"What is it you want to know?" he asked.

"I wanted to know, had she a lot of money to leave to—anyone? But I oughtn't to have asked. Good night."

He stopped her again. "Why do you want to know that?"

"I don't know. I mean, I know, but it was a silly question. I mean, it's never the amount by itself that counts as a motive for murder. All the same, she wasn't rich, was she? She never seemed to be."

"She certainly wasn't."

"Though with old people it's sometimes difficult to be sure. Sometimes they just don't care about spending money, and sometimes they're saving it all up for somebody else."

"I know she hadn't much to leave," Charles said. "She's been living for years on an annuity, which would come to an end at her death. So there's only the house and the things in it."

He saw relief in her eyes.

"Then that's all right," she said.

"Deborah, that's what Ivor said. What does it mean? Why do both of you think Peggie might have killed Aunt Alice for her money?"

But Deborah's eyes now showed fright and she turned and ran back to the house.

76

Slowly Charles started back to the house next door.

He wished that he had insisted on telephoning to Peggie himself and as soon as he had let himself into the house, he went to the telephone and asked the local operator for her number. Again he heard the telephone ring and ring in her flat. Again there was no answer. Suddenly wondering if in fact Ivor had spoken to her at all while he had been in his study, Charles slammed the instrument back on its stand and went upstairs to bed.

Until he got into bed he did not notice the silence of the house. Really it was no more silent than it would have been if Mrs. Robertson had been safely asleep in her bed, yet as soon as Charles's head touched the pillow, he began to feel that he had never in his life heard such a silence. The sighing of the wind in the chimney and the rattle of a window made it only the deeper. He felt cold in the comfortable bed, and he soon began to toss and turn with the restlessness of exhaustion.

An intense desire grew in him to go downstairs again and telephone to Sarah. He needed to hear her voice as he had never needed it before. It was a very attractive voice, calm and clear, with the soft Edin-burgh cadence. Merely to hear it just then, he felt, would take the ache out of his bones and the burning out of his brain. But to telephone a hard-working woman, who needed her sleep, at half-past one in the morning, would not be a kindness. He de-termined to master the impulse and with his eyes open, staring at the darkness, he tried to lie still.

He kept hearing Deborah asking him why he wanted his aunt's death to be a murder. When she had asked it, the question had seemed foolish and fantastic. But now in the new, deep silence of the house, his tired mind became confused and he began to wonder if she might not have been right. Why should he be so certain that Baldrey had shut the door to the attic? Why should it seem impossible that the wind had blown it open? Why, if it came to that, should it seem impossible that Mrs. Robertson had struggled to the top of the stairs and for some reason of her own, opened the door to the attic, then tripped and fallen when she was on her way downstairs again?

One answer to that last question was that she had been lying on her back. If she had fallen when she was facing down the stairs, she might have fallen on her face, or on her side, or in a crumpled heap, but surely it would have been very difficult for her to fall flat on her back.

Yet the police must have noticed that fact and they did not seem much impressed by it. So why should he be so sure that his aunt had been murdered?

He supposed that you could go all psychological about it, if you wanted to, and say that because of his neglect of her, he felt a certain guilt for her death, which he was trying very hard to unload on to someone else. He remembered thinking that there had been a note of accusation in Baldrey's voice when he had said that Mrs. Robertson was too much alone and would one day fall and hurt herself again. Well, had that note really been in Baldrey's voice, or had it only been a reverberation in Charles's own mind?

You could go on for ever on those lines, if you tried, and keep yourself awake all night and for many nights.

But suppose that he had been right about the door. Suppose that Alice Robertson, old, helpless, harmless, kind and loving, had been brutally killed and yet that no one but himself was going to believe it. Suppose

79

even Sarah, when he told her the whole story, would not believe it. Talk of responsibility!

At last he drifted into sleep, an uneasy sleep, haunted by dreams of footsteps overhead, of unanswered telephones, of still, dead white faces, amongst them the shining and ferociously grinning face of the White Lion, which swayed slightly, as if it were hanging from a gibbet.

Out of this sleep he was awakened suddenly by the knowledge that he had heard footsteps in his room.

# Chapter V

OPENING HIS eyes, he saw the dim shape of a face at the end of his bed.

As his head jerked up from the pillow, a woman's voice said, "Sorry if I startled you. The light doesn't seem to work."

Charles felt for the switch hanging behind the bed.

"That's because I turned it off here," he said as he sat up. "Hallo, Peggie."

She gripped the rail at the end of the bed with both hands and leant forward, staring at him intently. Her face, which, like his, was wide at the temples, with a high, broad forehead and a narrow, almost pointed chin, was very pale and there were purplish smears of anxiety under her eyes.

They were dark eyes, wide-spaced and observant. She was small and had always been slenderly built, but she looked even thinner now, Charles thought, than when he had gone away. She was wearing a camel-hair coat and a woollen scarf tied over her short, curly hair. Blinking at her in the light, seeing a wind-blown curl hanging over her forehead, he thought for a moment that she had bleached her hair, which was something that he would never have expected her to do, but then he realised that the truth was even more surprising. At the age of twenty-nine, Peggie's hair, which three years ago had been a dark, warm brown, was almost white.

It gave her an extraordinary look of distinction, almost of beauty, which was new. In Charles's memory of her she had had a cheerful, rather puppyish charm, destroyed from time to time by scowling moods of depression, which she had never hesitated to inflict on others with all the vigour of an excitable nature. But the young woman who was looking at him now had poise and dig-

81

nity and set a high value on controlling her feelings.

"I'm sorry I had to wake you up," she said, "but Ivor didn't really tell me much. So I thought the best thing was to drive straight down and talk to you. There's no need for you to get up. If you'll tell me just one or two things, I'll leave you in peace."

Her manner had a steely equanimity which Charles found more unnerving than tears.

"I'll tell you the whole thing, if you like," he said. "But in that case, sit down. It'll take me some time."

He wondered, as he said this, what Ivor had talked about on the telephone, if he had not told her much about the murder. But at least it was evident that he had actually spoken to her and that the reason why she had not answered when Charles had telephoned only a little later was that she had already started on her drive down here. It made his suspiciousness seem foolish and rather ugly.

She did not sit down, but kept her tight hold of the rail at the end of the bed.

"All right, but there are some things I want to ask before you begin," she said. "I know you'd come round to them sooner or later, but I'd prefer to know them at once."

"Go ahead, then," he said.

"Ivor said you believe that Granny was murdered."

"I do." Then he remembered his doubts of an hour or two ago, hesitated and added, "Yes, I do."

"Why was she murdered?"

"I don't know."

"Who do you think murdered her?"

"For God's sake, Peggie," he exclaimed, "do you seriously expect me to be able to answer that?"

"Why not?"

"How could I possibly—unless I'd done it myself?"

"I really want to know why you've got this fantastic idea of murder in your head at all. Ivor said he doesn't think the police agree with you."

"I don't think they do."

"He doesn't agree with you either."

"He doesn't really know anything about it. You'd better let me tell you the whole thing, then I think you'll understand."

She turned away to the window. Although the blank window-panes only mirrored the lighted room, she put her face close to them and stood staring out into the garden, as if she were able to see the trees and flower-beds down there in the windy darkness.

"I rather wish I didn't have to hear it," she said, "but I suppose I must."

Charles found that the droop of her head and shoulders betrayed her feelings far more than her stiff, formidable face and for the first time it occurred to him that he had done nothing so far to comfort her and that in this he had perhaps seriously failed her. Yet when he came to the end of his story, which he made as brief as he could, and then attempted to say that she was to count on him for any help that he could give her, she turned, giving him one swift, hard glance, and went to the door. He thought that she was going straight out of the room without speaking, but in the doorway she paused.

"Are you sure that David Baldrey was in the car when you came back from posting that letter?" she asked.

"Yes," Charles said.

"If it *was* murder then, he couldn't have done it. He wouldn't have had time to get here, go to the attic, come down, do a murder on the way and get back to the car in the time that it took you to post the letter."

"No."

"Then I think I believe, with the police and Ivor, it wasn't murder."

Her calm tone made Charles forget his sympathy for her.

"Why should Baldrey be the only possible murderer?" he asked. "I rather like him."

"How well do you know him?" she asked.

"Not well at all. But Aunt Alice did, and she liked him."

"I expect a lot of people have liked their murderers until the last minute. However, I admit Baldrey isn't a murderer—not if he was in the car. I only brought it up because I happen to find it very easy to think of him as a murderer. And as several other things."

"What other things? What have you got against him?"

"Let's leave all that till to-morrow. Good night, Charles. Sleep well and do try not to indulge your love of drama at everyone else's expense. Granny wouldn't have liked that, you know."

She went out quickly.

Charles did not sleep much more that night. Once or twice he dozed off, but was glad to awake from the dreams that crowded in upon him as soon as consciousness gave up the job of warding them off. His soundest sleep came after daylight was already pouring in at the window.

It was grey, discouraging daylight and when he woke again and lay there blinking at it, trying to summon up some enthusiasm for facing the new day, he saw raindrops spatter the glass. At the same time he heard from the garden a long scream, as if something were dying in agony. He bounded out of bed and in spite of the rain that drove into his face, wrenched up the heavy window and leant out.

He saw a cowboy and a Red Indian chasing each other round and round the cedar on the lawn. Both were screaming in unison, and now that he was fully awake, he recognised the noise as being of the kind produced for the sheer pleasure of screaming. From next door Deborah's voice, faint and ineffectual compared with those of her children, called to them to come in at once for their macs and gumboots, but it was plain that they saw no reason to take this seriously. A moment later the cowboy caught the Red Indian and the two of them fell sprawling on the wet grass, still yelling and hitting one another.

Charles pulled down the window, put on his dressing-gown, picked up his razor and toothbrush and went to the bathroom.

Going downstairs presently, he went to the kitchen and there found Mrs. Harkness, who had worked for Mrs. Robertson for many years, wandering aimlessly about in the kitchen, looking as if she thought that she ought to be busy, but not knowing where to start. She was talking softly to herself and from time to time putting the back of her hand to her eyes to wipe away the slowly welling tears. She made coffee for Charles and fried bacon and eggs and served them with stiff propriety in the big, cold dining-room. He was sitting there, trying to eat them, when Inspector Long, with the pink-faced sergeant following him, came quietly into the room.

Long said that he was sorry to intrude on Charles but something had come up and there was a question that he would like to ask him. Charles offered him and the sergeant coffee. They accepted it and sat down facing him across the broad table, at which as many as ten Robertsons at a time had been able to eat. Long drank his coffee eagerly and said that it was very acceptable. His manner was bland, yet under it he was tired and irritable, as if he thought that there was no real need for him to be there, talking to Charles, at all.

"The question I want to ask you," he said, "is about Mr. Baldrey. You told me that just after you arrived, you went upstairs and saw him come down the attic stairs and close the door at the bottom of them."

"Yes," Charles said.

"And that was at about six o'clock, I think."

"Yes, just about."

"In that case it was dusk."

"It was."

"Now, can you remember—this might be important, Mr. Robertson—whether or not Baldrey turned off the light at the bottom of the stairs?"

"I don't think the light was on," Charles said.

A flicker of annoyance showed in Long's eyes, "Are you quite sure about that? I'm talking about the light up in the attic. It's worked by a switch at the top of those stairs and another at the bottom."

Charles looked away into space, trying to visualise his meeting with Baldrey on the landing. It seemed to him that the small figure of the unknown man had loomed upon him out of the shadows. He had no memory of any dark silhouette against a light from above.

"Yes, I'm sure," he said. "Why, is it important?"

"Because Baldrey's fingerprints are on the lower switch as well as the upper and he himself says that he turned the light off at the bottom."

A memory stirred in Charles, floating up out of his unconscious but intimate knowledge of the house.

"Having turned it on at the top, do you mean?" he said. "He couldn't have done that, could he?"

"No, that's just the point, he couldn't," Long said. "All the wiring in this house is very old-fashioned, and although you can turn the attic light on either at the top or the bottom of the stairs, you've got to turn it off by the same switch. So he's told us something that can't be true."

"Aren't there any fingerprints besides his on the switch?" Charles asked.

"No," Long answered. "It's an old brass switch and it just happens that Mrs. Harkness polished it yesterday morning."

"But I still don't really see why it's important," Charles said. "It's easy to get muddled about a thing like that and if he turned it on on his way up, instead of at the top, as he thinks, and turned it off on his way down—"

"Ah!" Long said swiftly. "So you *aren't* sure the light upstairs wasn't on when you first saw him."

"Yes, I'm sure," Charles said. "I was just getting muddled myself. And come to think of it, he wouldn't have turned the light on when he arrived. That attic's got a good-sized window and he wouldn't have needed the light until a little while before he left."

Long gave an unwilling nod. "Yes, that's correct. And he hasn't said he turned the light on when he arrived. He says he turned it on upstairs when it got dark up there and then turned it off at the bottom. And that happens not to be possible."

"And what does that mean?"

"I haven't the faintest idea, Mr. Robertson. But you may remember I told you last night we would check for fingerprints in the attic, and if there were any which it was difficult to explain, we would investigate further. Well, Baldrey's prints on that switch are difficult to explain."

"But Baldrey was in his car down the lane when my aunt was killed."

"When she met her death, yes, so you told us."

Charles noticed Long's correction of his phrasing and a spark of anger began to glow in his mind. He wanted to assert that his aunt had been murdered and that tricks with phrasing would not alter that fact. But his own doubts of the night were still with him and he remained silent.

Long stood up. The sergeant stood up beside him.

"I understand Baldrey knew his way about the house pretty well," Long said. "Your aunt employed him a good deal, didn't she?"

"I think they were pretty good friends," Charles said. "She told me he'd helped her a lot since her accident."

"And then he found those things for her in the attic—the picture and those books?"

"Yes."

"And told her about them?"

"Of course."

"Telling her, however, that they weren't very valuable?"

"Not highly valuable, Inspector. He told

91

her they were probably worth three or four hundred pounds."

"I wonder . . ." Long began thoughtfully, but as he hesitated, seeming to change his mind about saying any more, the front-door bell rang.

Charles started towards the dining-room door to answer it, but as he did so Peggie came running down the stairs and made for the front door so swiftly that even if for some reason he had been eager to get there first, he could not have done so. He saw her face as she went by, curiously alight with the new, austere beauty that he had noticed the night before. With the strangeness of her silver curls clustering on her young forehead, the brilliance of her big eyes with the violet smears of strain beneath them, her tense, upright carriage and a black dress, which fitted her closely to the hips, then flared out in swinging folds, there was something, Charles thought, a little unearthly about her, a little uncanny.

With a quick movement she threw the door open.

When she saw David Baldrey standing diffidently on the doorstep, her whole manner changed. Some doubt seemed to be settled in her mind. Some uncertainty disappeared. Colour flooded her cheeks and in a high, clear, furious voice, she cried, "Go away and don't come back here! I don't want ever to see you in this house again!"

The startled pain and humiliation on Baldrey's face made Charles feel shrinkingly embarrassed. He said, "For God's sake, Peggie! Baldrey, come in."

Peggie stood in the way. "Be quiet, Charles. I said, I won't have him in here."

"I'm sorry," David Baldrey said. "I didn't know you minded my coming." With an effort that Charles could see, he was making himself look directly into Peggie's face. "I only came to ask if there was any way I could help. The offer still stands if you change your mind about me. Apart from that, I rather want a word with Mr. Robertson." He looked at Charles. "In the circumstances, would you mind a short walk with me? The rain isn't heavy."

Peggie ignored the fact that he had spoken to Charles. She swept on, "You've been helping so much about the place, Mr. Baldrey, that you may think you almost belong here. From what Mrs. Harkness has been telling me you've been coming and going pretty much as you liked. And you've come to know so much about us all that perhaps you've been feeling almost like one of the family. And that may have been how my grandmother thought about you in recent times. But I don't. I do hope you understand that. I don't at all."

Afraid that she might have still more to say, Charles turned quickly and spoke to Long. "Inspector, you don't need me any more, do you?"

He was thinking that Deborah had indeed been right when she said that Peggie had changed, and as this went through his mind, something that Mrs. Robertson had said added itself to Deborah's uncertain warning. Mrs. Robertson had spoken of what she had called a "dramatic something", which many of the less brilliant Robertsons possessed and which often seemed to go bad in them if they had no chance to stand up and perform and be admired. Charles had not thought at that time that she could be referring to Peggie. He had always taken for granted that she was one of the brilliant Robertsons. Relatively brilliant, anyway. You didn't have to put her alongside James, or even Frederick, to believe that in a few years' time, in her own limited field, you would hear her name spoken with a certain respect. Yet here she was, performing as hard as she knew how. Only why, and to what audience?

Long was tugging at his lower lip. He was not looking at Peggie, but past her and past David Baldrey into the garden.

"Well, now, that depends on who this is just arriving," he said. "It might be someone we'd both want to talk to, Mr. Robertson, and in that case, perhaps Mr. Baldrey wouldn't mind waiting."

Charles turned back to the door and looked out.

An old taxi from the nearby town had just drawn up at the gate. A man in a raincoat and wide-brimmed felt hat had just lifted out two suitcases and was paying the driver. He was fumbling with the money, as if it were something with which he was not familiar. As the taxi drove off, he turned towards the house, saw the group in the doorway, and advanced towards it.

As he did so, a shrieking Red Indian and a bellowing and threatening cowboy, both of them drenched with rain, came racing round the corner of the house and chose the newcomer as a handy object round which to chase one another. Their dirty hands clutched the spotless raincoat. Their feet splashed mud over the stranger's shoes. He smiled benevolently and said, "Now, that makes me feel really at home." Then he advanced to David Baldrey, held out a hand and said, "I can tell at a glance, sir, that you're a member of the Robertson family. My name's Harlan K. Stacey, and I'm very proud to know you."

# Chapter VI

BALDREY WENT scarlet, ignored the outstretched hand and bolted behind Inspector Long.

Charles came to the rescue, correcting Professor Stacey's mistake and introducing everyone present, including the two policemen. There was a pause as the American looked from one face to another, even in that difficult situation, Charles thought, looking for recognisable Robertson features. But the smile had left the professor's face, as if he had already reached the conclusion that the presence of the police indicated that the situation into which he had blundered was even more difficult than it appeared.

He had a plump face, pink and firm-fleshed, with clear blue eyes behind rimless spectacles. He was a short man with that air of buoyancy about him that plump people so often have. His hair was very fair and his eyebrows so pale that they were almost invisible.

In the end he looked back at Charles.

"It seems I may have arrived at an awkward time, sir," he said. "If so, I'll make my apologies and hope to be allowed to return later. I came to call on Mrs. Robertson. Mrs. Alice Robertson. She was expecting me, I believe, though possibly not so early in the day."

There was a question in his voice. Mrs. Robertson's absence from this group on the doorstep, which contained policemen, had already disturbed him.

Hesitantly Charles explained to him that he had not arrived too early but too late.

Deep distress appeared on the pink face. When Charles finished, Stacey muttered a few words of conventional condolence and then of apology for having intruded at such a time.

"Believe me, it's a great shock, a great personal loss to me as well," he said. "I've been in correspondence with Mrs. Robertson for a number of years and had come to think of her as a friend, a dear friend, although we had never met, and to meet her was the very first thing I wanted to do on arriving in Britain."

"I know she was looking forward very much to meeting you, Professor," Charles said. "I posted a letter to you from her only yesterday evening."

"A letter?" Stacey said. "Then she didn't get my telegrams? She didn't know I'd be arriving to-day?"

"A telegram arrived last night after her death," Charles said.

Stacey gave a bewildered little shake of his head. "It would have made no difference, in any case. And now it seems to me the best I can do is to get out of your way as quickly as possible. Maybe you could tell me of a hotel in the neighbourhood. If you could direct me to one, I should be most grateful."

This brought Peggie to herself. She had been glowering blindly at Stacey as if she did not see him. Now, for the first time, her eyes focused on his face instead of on some shadowy thing that she had seen beyond it.

"No, no, you must come in, Professor," she said. "My grandmother expected you. She—she'd never forgive us if we let you go away. For some reason we all thought it was next week-end you were coming, but I expect she muddled up the dates. But it makes no difference, does it? I mean . . ." She stopped with an air of helplessness. "Come in," she added with sudden brusqueness and turned back into the house.

Stacey exchanged an uncertain glance with Long, then followed Peggie inside. Charles would have followed too if Baldrey had not caught his arm and said in a low voice, "Are they sure—are they dead sure —it was accidental?"

Charles looked thoughtfully into his face.

"*I'm* not sure," he answered.

"But why not?" Baldrey's voice had gone hoarse. "Why should anyone do that to her? To her of all people?"

"I don't know yet. What makes *you* think it might be murder?"

"I don't, I don't. Because there'd have to be a reason. And there couldn't be one, could there? How could anyone have a reason to murder that old lady?"

"I believe reasons for murder don't always have to be particularly good reasons," Charles said.

"All right, all right then, say it was a burglar, a tramp, someone on the run, ready to do murder for a meal and a handful of loose change—and it was just bad luck he picked on her house. All right, that might make sense. But they don't believe that—not to go by all the questions they asked me about lights being turned on and off in the attic. They said it was an accident but they kept asking me questions. So what do they really believe, that's what I want to know."

"I don't know any more than you do," Charles said.

"She never did anybody any harm," Baldrey went on with the thin note of hysteria in his voice. "If she'd known anything bad about anyone, she'd have kept it to herself. She didn't depend on anyone who was sick of the burden. She'd nothing much to leave anyone. Those things I found in the attic, they aren't worth much—not enough. Loose change is one thing, but things like that picture and all have to be worth much more than those are to make someone do murder for them. But they've kept asking me whom I told about the things. I said, just Mrs. Robertson herself. But I don't know how many people she told about them and I wish to God, I said, I'd never told even her. She'd got on all her life without them."

Tears shone in Baldrey's eyes. Dropping his hold on Charles's arm, he walked rapidly away.

Rather startled by the discovery that the police appeared to be taking the possibility that Mrs. Robertson had been murdered more seriously than they had led him to imagine, Charles stood looking after the hurrying figure for a moment, then went back into the house.

He went to the sitting-room. He expected to find Peggie, Long and the American there, but instead he found Peggie alone. She gestured towards the dining-room.

"He's in there," she said, "being very politely asked what the hell he's really doing here."

"Hasn't he told us that already?" Charles said.

"Except why he turned up a week before he was expected."

"But you said yourself Aunt Alice must have muddled up the dates."

"That was just to be polite to him. She didn't do that sort of thing."

"Well, there's probably some quite simple explanation," Charles said. "The question is now, what are we going to do with

101

him? He's come a long way to see the Robertson relics."

"I asked him to stay here, didn't I?" Peggie said. "If he doesn't want to, that's his own business."

"He suggested a hotel, which seems to me a much more sensible idea," Charles said. "Is there a tolerable one anywhere near?"

"There's the White Lion, practically on the doorstep."

"That's just a country pub."

"Oh, not these days." Peggie had been pacing up and down the room, her full skirt swinging. Now she stood still, looking curiously at Charles. "You've actually stayed away quite a long time, haven't you? You don't know much about what's been going on here."

His eye had been caught by her dress, which, it seemed to him, would have been magnificent for a cocktail party, but here and now seemed outrageous, even if it was the only black dress that she possessed.

"I don't suppose I do," he said.

"The White Lion, for instance, is quite a smart place, with central heating and two new pink bathrooms," Peggie said. "It gives

102

you bad food, which it calls by French names, and you pay the earth for it."

"There've been some changes that I *have* noticed," he said. "One's in you, Peggie. You've changed a great deal since I went away."

He saw her hand stray to her grey hair, but he thought that the gesture was unconscious. Dropping into a chair, she leant back and met his eyes with a directness that seemed an effort.

Her voice was defensive. "One has to grow up, you know, sooner or later."

"You make it sound as if it's been rather unpleasant."

"It hasn't been outstandingly pleasant," she answered, "though I've been told I oughtn't to complain. And I don't. Usually."

"The job's all right?"

"The job's fine."

"What's wrong, then?"

"Ask me that again when I've had two or three drinks, Charles. This is the wrong moment."

"I suppose it is. Sorry." He sat down facing her. "Peggie, what have you got against David Baldrey?"

He saw her features twitch, then all the expressiveness died out of her face.

"I don't think I want to talk about it," she answered stiffly. "I—I may be prejudiced, perhaps, because I haven't much patience with the sort of man who can't make up his mind what to do with his life. He's quite an intelligent man and if only he'd stick at any job whatever, he could amount to something and not have to wheedle his way into the confidence of innocent old ladies by doing their plumbing and mending their fuses for them."

"You're forgetting——"

"Oh, I know exactly what you're going to say. You're going to say I'm forgetting his wartime experiences. Well, you had some wartime experiences too, didn't you, but you haven't ended up as a confidence man."

"That's a very serious thing to say," Charles said, "unless you've evidence of what you're saying. Have you any evidence, Peggie?"

"Oh, let's not go on talking about him."

Outside the door they heard footsteps and the voices of Long and Professor Stacey.

Charles went on quickly, "Those things Baldrey found in the attic—is there anything wrong with them? Are they fakes? Has he tried to make anything out of them?"

"No, no, no!" she said in a quiet, violent tone. "The only thing that's wrong with them is that they aren't worth much. Oh, God—" suddenly her features were contorted and pain erupted into her voice like blood bursting from the broken scab of a wound—"Oh, God, if only they were worth something!"

The next moment she was smiling calmly as Professor Stacey came into the room.

It was agreed without much discussion that he should take a room at the White Lion and that Charles should show him the way there. Stacey had two heavy suitcases, so Charles fetched his car from the garage and drove him the short distance. In the car, Stacey told him that his wife, who had set out that morning for Stratford on Avon, had taken their car, and that he felt a little anxious about her, since she was unused to driving on the left-hand side of the road.

"And our car naturally has a left-hand drive, which makes it harder," he said, sounding as if he were determined at any cost to make conversation that could not be painful. "If we'd been coming only to England, it would have made better sense to leave it at home and hire one for the time we were here, but we're going on to France, Switzerland and Germany and in all those countries it'll be fine. I've got six months' sabbatical leave, in which I hope to finish the book I'm writing on your ancestor, James Robertson, and our trip's been planned as nearly as possible to repeat a trip made by him in the year 1725 to visit Münzinger in Freiburg. Karl Münzinger, as you are certainly aware, influenced James Robertson deeply and they maintained a correspondence for many years. It's believed James also had a love-affair with Münzinger's daughter, though this is thought by some to be only a romantic tradition, arising from the fact that she was a woman of great beauty, who had a number of lovers, and who, very soon after Robertson's departure, retired to a convent."

The placid voice stopped as Charles drew up outside the White Lion. If anyone had asked him what the American had been talking about, he could not have repeated a single thing that had been said, for he had been thinking about Peggie and the frantic pain in her voice and on her face as she gasped out her amazing need for money. Amazing because she was Peggie, a serious-minded girl if ever there was one, with a good job, a promising career ahead of her and no known vices. Peggie whom he had known since before she could talk.

But three years is a long time. Plenty of time in which to develop new vices and even new virtues. Time too, perhaps, to have acquired a debt that must somehow, sometime, be paid, or a burden of tragedy from which money might seem to promise escape.

"Mr. Robertson," Stacey said, "I apologise again for intruding on your grief at this time, but since I've done so, will you come in here and have a drink with me and listen to a proposition I should like to make?"

Charles dragged his attention back to the man beside him.

"Thank you, but I think perhaps I ought to go back, once we've made sure they can fix you up here," he said.

"Let me explain," Stacey said, "it's on a matter which may be of the greatest importance to you and Dr. Robertson. Also, since I understand from my conversation with Inspector Long that there's a certain element of doubt as to how Mrs. Robertson met her death, I would add that some information in my possession might have some bearing on that problem."

"Well, in that case . . ."

"It needn't take us long," Stacey said, and they went together to the door of the White Lion.

The landlord came to meet them, a man so short as to be almost dwarfish, with the hollow chest and long, dangling arms of a hunchback. He had on a brown pin-stripe suit and suède shoes with thick, crêpe rubber soles. Sunk between his wide, deformed shoulders, a pale face with wary eyes looked up at his visitors with a bright, nervous smile.

He said that Stacey could certainly have a room, a nice room, was very welcome, had only to ask for anything he wanted, because that was what he himself, George Nutting, was here for, he was here simply to see that everyone had everything they wanted. Grasping Stacey's heavy suitcases as if they had no weight at all, he darted upstairs with them. Stacey followed, while Charles went into the bar to wait for him.

It had once been a simple, frowsy little room with lace curtains and a few old flyblown advertisements. Now it was all horse-brasses and pewter. When Charles entered,

no one else was there, but as he sat down on one of the oak settles that had replaced the creaking but more comfortable basket-chairs, a girl appeared through a door behind the bar and asked him what he wanted to drink. He answered that he would wait for his companion. She nodded and withdrew. She had closed the door behind her and Charles was fumbling his way back to his interrupted, startling thoughts about Peggie, when he was brought up short by the realisation that the girl who had come in, spoken to him and gone out again, was almost certainly Jean Baldrey.

She had been a small girl, slender, dark, soft-spoken. Charles had not really taken in much about her except her attractive, low-pitched voice. She had been an actress, he remembered, and perhaps some training had improved it. An unsuccessful actress, turned barmaid. He was watching the door behind the bar, waiting with curiosity for the girl to return, when Stacey came in and sat down beside him.

"I may be mistaken," Stacey said, as h tried to arrange his plump body comfortab on the narrow seat of the settle, "but seemed to me probable, a few minutes a to judge by your expression while I was t:

ing about the Münzingers, that you were finding it difficult to produce an appearance of interest in what I was saying. You've probably been familiar with the story all your life and found it both impertinent and ridiculous in me to attempt to instruct you. Alternatively, you had other things on your mind."

"That was the trouble," Charles said. "I know nothing about Münzinger except, very vaguely, that he was some sort of naturalist. I ought to explain, perhaps, that my scientific education stopped at that obsolete examination, the School Certificate."

"And you thought I was chattering with the frivolity of my monomania. As no doubt I was, in part. Mrs. Stacey tells me I'm capable of bringing the Robertson family in to explain anything from Newtonian dynamics to a game of bridge. She warns me I shall probably end up believing myself to be James Robertson. Mrs. Stacey is a very wonderful person, objective, tolerant and supremely well adjusted. If she had come here with me I should have asked her advice before saying to you what I am about to say now. But she preferred to spend her first days in Britain in Stratford on Avon. And

the truth is, I do have specialised knowledge, as well as a monomania."

The door behind the bar opened again and the girl reappeared. Lifting a flap in the bar, she came towards the two men and asked again what she could bring them to drink. Charles had no doubt now that she was Jean Baldrey. She and David Baldrey were sufficiently alike for there to be no question about it, even though she was so much the younger that it was strange to realise that they were brother and sister. She could not have been more than twenty-five. Her colouring was darker than his and her features were smaller and finer, but the two of them had come out of the same mould and both had the same rather disturbing air of possessing more intelligence than they quite knew how to use.

When she had brought Stacey and Charles the beer that they ordered, she went back behind the bar and stayed there to polish glasses and rearrange bottles on a shelf, and also, as Charles saw, to listen intently. He wondered if he ought to point this out to Stacey.

"What I have to say," Stacey continued, "has mainly to do with Franziska Münzinger, although the relationship between

111

James Robertson and her father is also of interest to us. They corresponded—we know that—for several years before Robertson paid his visit to Freiburg. We know it because Robertson was an orderly man who kept his correspondence, and Münzinger's letters mostly survive. They were sold by Christina Robertson, the oldest of Frederick Robertson's daughters, to a countryman of mine, John J. Meinetwegen, and are now in the famous Meinetwegen collection. She obtained, I'm sorry to say, a fantastically small sum for them, appearing to have had no conception of the value of what she was selling. Except when her more intelligent sisters prevented it, she appears to have sold or given away, as if they were worthless, any family relics on which she was able to lay her hands. Possibly this was a way of expressing revolt against her father, who had prevented her marriage to a penniless young poet, who thereupon gave up poetry, left for Australia and made a great deal of money, but never returned for Christina. I confess to a certain sympathy for Christina, particularly as I have never found the character of your great-grandfather sympathetic. In his own way, with more knowledge and therefore with less excuse,

I believe him to have been an even greater vandal than his daughter."

"I've never felt greatly attracted by him myself," Charles said, "but my cousin Peggie will tell you he did some important work."

Stacey nodded and drank some beer.

"I'm talking a great deal too much," he said. "If Mrs. Stacey were here, she would keep me within limits. She has a wonderfully clear mind and can always keep me to the point. As it is, I've strayed right away from Münzinger and the influence he exerted through his letters on young James Robertson, at the time when he was first developing his theory of ideal morphological forms. I've had the privilege of editing those letters and sometimes through them one catches a glimpse of the sort of man James must have been. But we know nothing of what he wrote to Münzinger. James's letters vanished. It has generally been supposed that they were destroyed by Franziska before she took the veil, or that they had been just plain lost. You are certainly acquainted with those conscienceless women who throw things away simply because they don't care for litter. Have you ever thought of all the history that's been sacrificed to the mere habit of neatness of some brainless house-wife, reaching out with her broom and dust-er to deprive the future of its heritage?"

Stacey coughed and gave an apologetic smile.

"Excuse me, Mr. Robertson, I have de-livered this lecture rather often. To cut it short, let me state that I do not believe in the theory of the over-zealous housewife or servant. I believe that Franziska was to blame for Robertson's priceless letters hav-ing been lost, but I do not believe that she destroyed them. For reasons which I shall give you, I have come to believe she re-turned them all to James Robertson, before burying her beauty in the convent."

"In that case, I suppose it was James him-self who destroyed them," Charles said.

"Ah, no," Stacey said quickly. "Not nec-essarily. It's my own belief that those letters may still exist. I believe, unless the unfor-tunate Christina laid her misguided hands upon them, that they may still be some-where in that house built by Frederick Rob-ertson more than a century later."

At last Charles's interest was roused. It had always been easy to set his imagination in a blaze with the name of James Robertson. He found now that it needed an effort to remain sceptical.

"You said you'd reasons for this belief of yours," he said. "Are there really any reasons?"

"Good reasons, Mr. Robertson," Stacey said. "It would be unscholarly at this point to claim they're conclusive reasons. Nothing but the discovery of the letters themselves will prove me a hundred per cent right. But there's enough evidence that the letters exist to warrant a very careful search for them in that house. Mr. Robertson—" Stacey cleared his throat with a new sound of nervousness—"Mr. Robertson, I should regard it as a very great privilege to be allowed to take part in such a search."

"But this evidence you mentioned . . ."

Stacey leant towards him. "Mr. Robertson, that evidence comes to us from Frederick himself, in a letter he wrote to his nephew, Robert MacIntyre, the surgeon, whose son emigrated to Canada and whose descendants are now to be met with in various parts of the American continent. One of them, a Mrs. Whitfield, happens to be in possession of the whole correspondence between Frederick and Robert MacIntyre and she granted me the privilege of studying it. The experience, I must admit, was not wholly pleasurable, since Frederick, if you will allow me to say so, was far from entertaining as a letter writer. Yet embedded in the solid, well-nigh impenetrable rock of his prose style, I found treasure."

Stacey put a hand in a pocket and brought out a note-book. As he did so, he gave Charles another quick smile.

"This is merely a formality," he said. "I know these words by heart. But here they are, as I noted them on November the nineteenth of last year, when I first read them. 'I have followed your advice,' Frederick wrote, 'and have not destroyed *those papers.*' Those last two words are heavily underlined. He was almost as addicted to that habit as Queen Victoria herself. He continues, 'It may be, as you argued, that a later generation will take a more lenient view than ours of what I found so painful to read and so distressing, nay, so unbearable to associate with a *name so great.*' More underlining. 'However, I have put the letters in a place of concealment, from which I pray they may not be recovered during my lifetime, or in those of my daughters. Above all, I pray that my son Lancelot may never

116

set eyes upon them, for he is, I fear, capable of selling them *for profit.'*"

Stacey snapped the note-book shut and slapped it down on the table before him.

"Now to what could he have been referring if it was not to the private papers of James Robertson?" he demanded. "And let me add that that letter to MacIntyre was written just one week after Frederick had sold his house in Cambridge and moved to the new house which he had built for himself on his retirement. You understand the significance of that, of course. When one moves house after fifty years in one place, one disturbs the accumulations of a lifetime. One disturbs the dust—in his case—of generations. And in those rare cases where a sense of family has been sufficiently strong, where possessions from the past have been treasured over many generations and somehow escaped the depredations of the unspeakable Christinas, why should not letters written very long ago indeed come to light? And having done so——"

"Wait a minute!" Charles said. "Having done so, why should one promptly hide them away again? Frederick was a sound scientist, even if he wasn't in the same class as James, and if he'd happened on the letters

James wrote to Münzinger, he'd have known all about how important they were, and been wild with excitement and pride. Yet, according to you, his first thought was actually to destroy them. That doesn't make sense. It isn't thinkable."

"Isn't it? Not even when you remember that Frederick was an elderly mid-Victorian and James, when he wrote those letters, a young man of his own century, passionately in love? And when you remember that Frederick almost certainly found not only the letters James wrote to Münzinger, but also those that he had written to Franziska, a woman not very young and not very innocent, to whom explicitness in a love-letter would not have been unwelcome? Why, Frederick's cheeks would have burnt with shame. He would have seen the letters, not as poetry, but as the eternal tarnishing of a great name. The wonder is that he didn't rush straight to the nearest fireplace with them but actually brought himself to discuss them with his very respectable nephew, Robert MacIntyre, who fortunately had some sense, as a result of which the letters were hidden—for us, I hope, to find. Oh, I do most earnestly and sincerely hope so, Mr. Robertson."

Stacey's voice dropped, became deeply agitated and humble.

"For me it would be the crown of a lifetime of work, the perfect climax. And for you and Dr. Robertson—well, if you consider the probable mixture in those letters of profound thought and eroticism, of philosophy and romance, of sex and science, and also the alteration in public taste that has indeed taken place since Frederick's time—oh, I think it may safely be said that for you they'd be . . . ." Stacey's excitement could not be restrained. "Boy, they'd be a goldmine! They'd be oil! They'd be uranium!"

A glass slipped out of the hands of the girl behind the bar. It was thick glass. It did not break, but thudded dully on the floor. She stood quite still for a moment, then, with a curious, stunned slowness, stooped to pick it up, then went out quietly, closing the door behind her.

# Chapter VII

CHARLES GOT to his feet. The behaviour of Jean Baldrey had distracted him. He found it extraordinarily hard for the moment to concentrate on Stacey. With his eyes on the closed door, he said vaguely, "I'll tell my cousin what you've told me, Professor, and I've no doubt she'll ask you to come and help in a search."

"Thank you, Mr. Robertson."

"But even if you're right, there's something I still don't understand. You said your information might have bearing on my aunt's death—if it wasn't an accident. You mean, I suppose, that these letters would be so valuable that they'd provide a convincing motive for an otherwise incomprehensible murder."

"Yes, indeed."

"But wouldn't that mean that someone besides yourself deduced their existence? Or found them and didn't let on?"

"Yes, and then returned to steal them."

"But that's just the trouble. Why did he choose such a perilous time to come back and collect them? I'd only gone out for a short walk to post a letter. Why didn't he wait until I'd gone back to Edinburgh and my aunt was alone?"

"Because it was then or never."

"Why?"

"Because I was coming."

"But you weren't expected till next

120

week," Charles said. "My aunt had muddled up the dates."

Stacey gave a slight shake of his head. "I know that's what Dr. Robertson said. But surely Mrs. Robertson received my first telegram—not the one I sent last night from London, but the one I sent off three days ago, as soon as we landed, when Mrs. Stacey and I resolved certain disagreements as to how we should spend our time in Britain by deciding to go our different ways. To be candid, I hadn't expected that concession from her and had been prepared to go to Stratford on Avon, or Stonehenge, or anywhere else she might choose, so long as we then came on to visit Mrs. Robertson. So the date I'd first suggested for my visit was a week hence, but on Mrs. Stacey pointing out to me that she lives with the Robertson family for three hundred and sixty-five days every year, and that our very secure and satisfactory relationship was hardly likely to be damaged if she were to take a short vacation from my work, I felt free to come here at once. Accordingly, I sent a telegram from Southampton, proposing the change of date and asking Mrs. Robertson, if this should be inconvenient, to notify me at our

121

London hotel. Since I received no answer, I assumed all was well and came."

"You know," Charles said, "I don't think my aunt ever got that first telegram."

"I believe it was addressed correctly."

"But if someone else took it over the telephone and then didn't tell her . . ."

Two people, Charles thought, might have had the opportunity to do that. The most obvious was Mrs. Harkness. But to Mrs. Harkness a telegram was always a matter of such importance that it was as difficult to imagine her forgetting to mention one to Mrs. Robertson as it was to believe her capable of deliberately suppressing the fact of its arrival. The other person who had the run of the house was David Baldrey.

Suddenly in a hurry, Charles said goodbye to Stacey and started home. He wanted to talk to Peggie. He wanted to find out what she thought of Stacey's theory of the letters, and also to make her tell him what it was that she had against Baldrey. For although he could not be the murderer, since Charles himself was witness to the fact that he had been in the car, waiting for his sister, when Mrs. Robertson had fallen to her death, he could have taken Stacey's telegram over the telephone and then told someone else about it. And in that case, any knowledge that Peggie might have about Baldrey, and perhaps about that small, dark girl who had eavesdropped so intently, and about their friends, could be vital.

Charles found Peggie at the garden gate. He thought that she was waiting for him, so he said, "I'm sorry I've been so long, but that man's just been telling me one of the most fantastic yarns I've ever listened to. And because it just might be true, I'd better tell it to you. Come on, let's go in."

She stared at him blindly, shook her head and said, "Presently."

"It's important," he said.

"All right, I'll come in a moment."

Charles went into the house. Later, when he remembered that encounter at the gate, he realised that all that day Peggie had been waiting for something. From the moment when he had seen her come running down the stairs to open the door to David Baldrey, she had been all nervous expectation, all impatience. But at the time, going to the sitting-room and pouring out two glasses of sherry, one for Peggie and one for himself, Charles noticed only his own impatience at her delay in coming to join him.

After a quarter of an hour he went out to

look for her. She was no longer at the gate and her car had gone from the garage. Fuming, Charles went inside and sat down alone to the sausages and mashed that Mrs. Harkness cooked for him.

For form's sake, he asked her if she knew of any telegram that had come for his aunt three days ago. She burst into a flood of speech, but it was all about the funeral and the fact that she had no black stockings. But perhaps, she said, that didn't matter nowadays, only she did want to do what was right. She seemed to have been brooding most of the morning on her stockings. In between her remarks on the subject, she made it plain that she had no knowledge of any telegram.

Charles did not succeed in talking to Peggie until late in the afternoon. If he had known how long it would be before she returned, he might not have waited for her, but have gone to find Baldrey without talking to her first. Waiting, however, thinking that she might come back at any moment, a need to talk to someone, to share the load that was piling up on his mind, became a little more than he could bear and, although he had almost no hope of finding Sarah at home on a Saturday afternoon, he picked up the telephone and asked for her number.

Her landlady told him that, as he had feared, Miss Inglis was away to Gullane to play golf. Charles rang off and since he could not talk to Sarah, settled down to write to her instead.

In a few minutes he had forgotten his impatience to talk to Peggie. Sarah that afternoon was good company, soothing and responsive. She was level-headed, understanding and grasped in a flash all that he was trying to say. Point by point, her image in his mind agreed with him and reassured him that on the whole he was acting for the best. His knowledge that Sarah in the flesh sometimes seemed to disagree with him even more often than she agreed, did not disturb his confidence in her. More fully than he ever had before, he realised that he knew where he was with her and that his feeling of trust in her was the best thing that he had known in his life.

He did not even hear Peggie come in. It was only when he went out to the hall, meaning to post his letter straight away, that he found her at the bottom of the staircase, waiting for him.

She had been crying. Her eyelids were

red and her lips were puffy. Her short silver curls were dishevelled and she was clutching a sodden handkerchief between her hands. But she still wore the black dress with the flaring skirt, which emphasised every curve of her body and every movement that she made.

That she had cried at least once for her grandmother reassured Charles, but the dress enraged him.

"For God's sake, can't you change that dress?" he exclaimed.

She looked bewildered and said, "It's the only one I've got here."

"You mean you deliberately put that on . . ."

"Don't be a fool. It's what I was wearing. I just put on my coat and came."

"But I thought you'd been having a bath when Ivor telephoned."

"Is that what he told you? The damn' fool. I'd been to a party."

"Did you tell him that?"

"Of course. Or didn't I? I can't remember. If I did, it looks as if he didn't believe me."

Charles thought that she was going to start crying again, which unnerved him, because he did not think that he had seen

Peggie cry since she was a child, and then it had usually been from temper.

"Can't you really remember if you told him or not?" he asked.

"Yes, I can now. I told him to mind his own business. That was because he asked where I'd been before he told me about Granny, then somehow I don't think we got back to it again. So he told you I'd been having a bath?"

"Because both the police and I had tried to telephone you earlier, and didn't get an answer."

"So he thought I might need an alibi and, out of the goodness of his heart, invented one for me, then forgot to tell me about it. How touching and how unspeakably like him! Was he drunk at the time?"

"Fairly."

She gave a helpless shake of her head. She looked exhausted and forlorn.

"I *was* at a party, Charles. Not that I see why that matters. There's something horrible about the way we keep edging up to talking as if Granny were murdered. All the same, I told the police all about it."

"Of course, Peggie."

"Don't you believe I was at a party?"

"A party means plenty of witnesses, so

I'd be stupid not to," he said. "Now, let's go into the sitting-room. There's something I want to tell you about Professor Stacey and it's quite a long story."

It was a story that he had just written to Sarah and he found himself telling it in almost the same words. But the feelings that developed in him as he told it now were remarkably different from those that had accompanied the writing of the letter. He had been extraordinarily convinced, all the time that he had been writing, of the truth of Stacey's theory, but throughout this second telling that conviction slowly died. Peggie listened quietly and attentively, but he became sure, long before he had finished, that when he stopped, she would laugh at him for even having thought this fantasy important enough to repeat.

She said nothing at first when he stopped, then she did laugh. It was an abrupt, excited laugh.

"It's a beautiful theory!" she said. "Oh, yes, it's beautiful."

"It's idiocy," Charles said, now completely convinced that it was.

"Oh, as to that . . ." She made an ambiguous gesture. "Yet how it hangs together. It's all so perfectly in character.

You've got Frederick Robertson, with his sober reputation and his respectable daughters and his enormous pride in his descent from James Robertson, who naturally had to be respectable too to be a fitting ancestor for them all. And then he turns out all of a sudden to have been a human being as well as a genius—and a human being of his own time, and not Frederick's. And then there's the fact that Frederick mentioned the papers in the letter to MacIntyre just after he and his daughters had moved away from the old house in Cambridge—that fits in wonderfully neatly and convincingly. And, lastly, the touch that the letters had to be hidden because Great-grandfather Lancelot might actually have thought of publishing them and so brought discredit to the great name and shame on them all." Peggie's tear-stained face was alight. "Yes, that's what I call a beautiful theory."

"There probably isn't a word of truth in it," Charles said warningly.

She might not have heard him. With her hand impetuously sketching lines in the air, she went on, "And Christina's an important part of it. Poor Christina, with her mania for getting rid of everything, or hiding away anything that reminded her of her father. Because if she hadn't done that, Granny, sometime in the spring cleanings of a lifetime, would have come across the letters . . ." Her hand dropped into her lap and the light went out of her face. "Charles, how I wish she had! She adored the whole Robertson business and it would have been about the most wonderful thing that ever happened to her."

"Look, Peggie——"

Up flew her hand again. "Oh, I know, I know. Facts or just daydreams? We'll come to that presently. Let's get back to Christina now. The question is, did she get rid of the papers or just hide them? If she got rid of them, there's nothing we can do but give Professor Stacey our blessing if he goes on trying to track them down. But if she hid them, we can make a pretty good guess at where they are, can't we?"

"I don't see——"

"They're in the attic, Charles. I told you, if they'd been anywhere else, Granny would have found them. But there's junk up there that hasn't been moved for half a century. That's where they've got to be."

"Peggie, they haven't got to be anywhere except in the imagination of Harlan K. Stacey."

Her face froze with anger. "Oh, haven't you any imagination yourself? No, I suppose you haven't, because if you had, you'd never have got yourself stuck in insurance. All the same, couldn't you, just for once, try to imagine what it could mean if—*if,* that's all I'm saying!—the man's right and those wonderful things are up there in the attic? And I'm not thinking of their financial value either. I'm thinking of what it would feel like to hold in my own hands letters that were written by James Robertson to Karl Münzinger and his daughter."

"All right," Charles said reluctantly. "But aren't you forgetting something? Even if those letters were up in the attic until yesterday evening—*they aren't there now!*"

She was silent for a moment, then said quietly, "Charles, nobody but you believes that Granny was murdered."

"Oh, don't they!"

"They'd never even have thought of it if you didn't keep bringing it up."

"Then why did Ivor invent an alibi for you?"

"He was drunk, wasn't he?"

"Yes, but not incapable."

"He's always a bit incapable and terribly easily influenced, even when he isn't drunk.

But suppose—suppose you're right and that Granny was killed because she caught somebody stealing the letters—we know who it was, don't we? And sometime we'll get the letters back again."

"You mean David Baldrey," Charles said in intense exasperation. "Peggie, he's the one person it couldn't have been. Even someone with an imagination much more elastic than mine wouldn't be able to stretch it to the point of believing that Baldrey could be in two places at the same time. Further, if he'd found the things and wanted to steal them, he could have done it whenever he felt like it—yesterday afternoon, for instance."

"Unless he wasn't quite certain yet what they were." Peggie got up and went to the door. "Well, are you coming with me to hunt for them?"

Charles stood up, started to follow her, then stood still. Her words had given him a shock. He remembered Baldrey speaking of his daydream that one day he would unearth a real treasure and have the knowledge to recognise it. Charles also remembered thinking that there had been something odd about his manner at the time. Baldrey's talk had been friendly, yet his face had been blank and secretive. He had been eager to know what Mrs. Robertson intended to do with the picture and the books that he had found for her, and had seemed relieved to hear that she had no thought of selling them. He had emphasised how little they were worth, had suggested that even that little might be subject to estate duty and that it might be best for her not to say too much about their having been found. Had that been because he wanted to discourage interest in his finds, wanted other people who might be capable of recognising a treasure to leave them alone, until he had made sure of what he had found?

"I'll come with you, Peggie," Charles said, "but first I want you to tell me something. What have you got against Baldrey? Is he a crook?"

From the doorway she answered indifferently, "That's such a definite word. Everyone's a bit of a crook, in my opinion, including you and me."

"I'm talking about theft in particular," Charles said. "Has he ever stolen anything from you?"

"Not exactly."

"Whatever does that mean?"

She considered the question, then answered guardedly. "He stole a confidence from me and traded it to someone else. That doesn't make him a crook in your sense, does it? It wasn't criminal. But it wasn't very nice, either. And I'm rather inclined to think him capable of almost anything. Now let's go upstairs and get started."

"But oughtn't Stacey to be in on it?"

"If the letters are there," she answered, "I think I'd sooner that you and I found them."

"But I practically promised him he could come and help with it," Charles said. "Damn it, he's come a long way just for that, and the whole thing's his idea."

"Which is just why I'd sooner search without him."

"I don't get it."

Slowly and distinctly, as if she were speaking to her least intelligent student, Peggie said, "We don't really know anything about him, do we, Charles? Even Granny didn't really know anything. Well, suppose he isn't quite what he seems. And even if he is, scholars aren't always the most honest people in the world. They've been known to turn crooked, just like other people. And suppose he's got a handsome set

134

of forged documents all ready to discover in the junk in the Robertson attic, which would make them so very much more convincing than if they turned up somewhere in America, would you really like him to get away with it?"

Charles did not trust himself to answer. Anger smouldered in him, but whether it was because of Peggie's suspicion of Stacey, or because he himself had not thought of it before her, he could not have said for certain.

He followed her up to the attic. At first he only stood watching while she searched, but after a few minutes her silent, feverish excitement spread to him and making his way towards a monumental roll-top desk in a corner, stepping over some rolls of old linoleum and between a rusty iron stove and a dressmaker's model many sizes too large ever to have been used by Alice Robertson, he began opening and closing the drawers of the desk.

There was nothing in them but dust, cobwebs and a few dead spiders.

But by then the mania of the hunt was upon him and he was practically convinced that within the next ten minutes he would have found the long lost letters of James

Robertson, inestimably precious to the scientist, the historian, the poet, and incidentally worth a good many thousands of pounds. He was not quite clear whether any of those thousands of pounds would belong to him, or whether they would all be Peggie's, but the mere thought of them was exciting.

He tried looking for the letters in the iron stove. Lifting out the heavy metal disc at the top, he struck a match and lowered it through the hole. Inside he found only more dust, cobwebs and dead spiders. Next he up-ended the massive dressmaker's model and peered among the wires under the covering of canvas. There was nothing there. Then he tugged at the lid of a tin trunk and as the hinges gave a rusty shriek he caught his breath, seeing a number of small white faces with glassy eyes staring up at him. The trunk, for how many years he did not know, had been a coffin for forgotten dolls.

Peggie was on her knees beside the trunk which, Charles remembered, had been open, with some books on the floor beside it, when he had come up here the evening before. She was taking out each volume, ruffling its pages, feeling its binding. When the trunk was empty, she gave a sigh of disappointment, then started feeling the sides and bottom of the trunk. At last, reluctantly, she began packing the books into it again.

After that, she started examining the roll-top desk which Charles had already searched. She was not content with merely looking into the drawers and pigeon-holes, but took all the drawers out of the desk and looked in the spaces behind them, tapping and measuring the partitions.

Presently she said, "You know, to do this thoroughly would take us a month."

"That thought isn't new to me," Charles answered.

"All the same, up here is where they've got to be."

"Or to have been."

She sat down on a chair with a broken back. It was of cherry wood and might have been worth repairing.

"If that's really what you believe," she said, "who do you think took them? You won't hear of its having been Baldrey. Well, who else could it have been?"

"Someone to whom Baldrey talked," he said.

"And who could that have been?"

"I've been wondering if you mightn't have some idea."

"Is that a way of hinting that it might have been me?"

He hurled to the ground an empty shoe-box, stored for heaven knew what reason.

"It's a way of saying that you seem to know something about Baldrey which you're keeping to yourself," he said. "Who does Baldrey talk to? Do you know anything about that? There's his sister, of course, but if she was working in the pub till ten o'clock, and then I suppose had to do some clearing up and so on, she couldn't have got up here to steal some papers and murder Aunt Alice any more than he could. Well, who else is there? Who are his friends?"

"I never heard of his having any," she answered.

"Whom did he go to with the confidence he got out of you?"

Peggie gave an odd smile. "I think it would surprise you considerably if I told you, but I'm not going to. It couldn't have anything to do with all this, in any case. Meanwhile, in case you've any doubts about that party I was at, and in case you've been turning over in your mind what I said about needing money, let's get back to me. Suppose I knew the letters were up here, and suppose I wanted them, don't you realise I'd only got to go to Granny and tell her so? The problem, if they'd been found while she was alive, would have been to *stop* her giving them to me. Don't you know that?"

He nodded. "Yes, I suppose that's true."

"Of course it's true."

"But I never suggested it was you who took the things," he said.

"Well, then, who did?"

He turned away to a chipped, painted chest of drawers which he vaguely remembered as having once been in the nursery, and said dispiritedly, "Oh, let's go on hunting."

Peggie got up and went back to the trunk full of books that she had already examined.

"Charles, these books are the ones that Baldrey found and told Aunt Alice about— the Proceedings of the Royal Society for the years 1864–1894. And they're the only things that show any signs of having been disturbed."

"What does that mean, except that Baldrey naturally examined them?" he asked.

"I don't know," she said. "But, as it happens, the run isn't complete. There's one volume missing."

"If you're thinking that perhaps Baldrey found the Robertson treasure in one of those books and thought of stealing it, once he'd made sure what it was, that won't work," Charles said, "because in that case, he'd hardly have told Aunt Alice about the books."

She rubbed her forehead with the back of a dusty hand, leaving a smudge of dirt there.

"People aren't always reasonable," she said.

"You still think it was Baldrey, don't you?"

She gave a deep sigh and said, "Oh, I don't know what I think. Let's go on searching."

But an hour later there was still no sign of any letters from James Robertson to Franziska Münzinger, or to Karl Münzinger, or to anyone at all. The light was failing and the attic becoming full of eerie shadows. It felt cold, wintry and unreal. The quest for the letters had become an absurdity.

Going to the top of the stairs, Charles turned on the light. As he did so, Peggie first swore, then threw down a piece of moth-eaten carpet felt which she had been not very hopefully examining, slammed shut the door of an empty cupboard and said, "For God's sake let's go downstairs and have a drink!"

Charles thought it the most sensible thing that she had said that afternoon.

"I'm not giving up," she went on, "but I'm tired and I'm frozen. Meanwhile . . ." She went back to the trunk of books, from which her attention had never strayed for long, and stooping suddenly, she took out a volume and tucked it under her arm.

"What's that for?" Charles asked.

"I think I'll go up to London this evening," she said. "I'd like to show it to someone I know. And that portrait too. Haven't papers sometimes been hidden behind pictures? Apart from that, though, it might be instructive to find out what this lot are actually worth."

"Baldrey said they aren't worth a great deal."

"That's what I want to check."

"It won't help you to find the Robertson papers."

"Did I say it would?"

She went down the stairs ahead of him.

They had their drinks in a bad-tempered silence. Both were nervous, more oppressed by their disappointment than they would admit to one another. Charles thought that Peggie probably felt as he did, that they had both been deluded by a pure fantasy of the American professor's, and that they looked rather foolish. When Peggie had finished her drink, muttered again that she was off to London and might or might not return that night, as she happened to feel inclined, and had gone, Charles found it a relief to be alone again.

He ate the cold meal that Mrs. Harkness had left prepared, then went out to his car. He drove past the White Lion to the corner by the letter-box and there posted his letter to Sarah. Then he turned down the lane that led to the Baldrey farm. He had decided that the simplest way to obtain information about David Baldrey was to go and ask Baldrey himself for it.

In the darkness the Baldrey farmhouse was invisible from the road, for it stood at the end of a drive cut through a belt of trees and bushes. In the daylight the roof and chimneys would have shown between the trees, but now the house and the farm buildings near it had faded into shadow.

Charles turned his car in at the gate, which was open and which, as he saw when his headlight slid across it, was too broken down ever to be closed, or moved at all from where it sagged amongst nettles and rank grass. His wheels jolted over deep ruts and skidded on mud. Reaching the house, he found a light shining through the panes of glass in the front door, and Baldrey's car in the yard before it.

Charles stopped his car behind the other, got out and went up to the door. When he was close to it, he saw how the paint had flaked away, leaving the wood almost bare. He saw too how weeds had sprouted between the paving stones of the yard, and how a climbing rose, trained up a trellis against the front of the house, had fallen away, dragging half the trellis with it. Things had not been like this in the old Baldreys' time. Wondering why, if they could do no better with the place than this, the young Baldreys had not sold it and gone away, Charles knocked at the door.

There was no answer. He knocked again several times. Because of the light in the passage and the car in the yard, he felt certain that Baldrey must be at home, yet all his knocking produced not the slightest sound of movement in the house. It was plain that Baldrey, if he was there, had decided not to answer.

There was nothing that Charles could do about it. Probably, he thought, Baldrey had seen him coming, had known that it was to ask him a number of awkward questions and had rapidly decided that he had already had more than enough of that at the hands of Inspector Long. On the other hand, perhaps he had not been at home at all. Getting into his car again, Charles decided to try telephoning when he got in, and if he had no luck at first, to try again several times during the evening. For if Baldrey was out, but was going to meet his sister as usual at the White Lion, he would have to return home for his car.

The telephone calls produced no result. Charles considered walking down the lane to look for Baldrey in the gateway where he had waited the evening before, but the thought that they would probably be interrupted almost immediately by Baldrey's sister, made him decide against this. Giving up the idea of talking to Baldrey that evening, he settled down with a drink by the fire.

When he first sat down there in the big, quiet room, his mind was full of Baldrey, of Stacey, of Peggie, and of the fruitless search in the attic. But presently he found himself thinking of Alice Robertson and of what she would have done if she had lived to listen, probably in this room, to Stacey's theory.

She would have told him to go ahead, of course. She would never have suspected his motives. She would have told him to search the house from top to bottom, to do anything he liked and have a good time. That would have been very important to her, that he should enjoy his long-awaited trip to England. But there would have been a glint of laughter in her dark little eyes, and dry, almost imperceptible mirth in her voice. And if he failed to find the precious papers, as Charles and Peggie had failed that afternoon, she would have hunted through her possessions for something to comfort him with, sending him away, perhaps, with a little blue and gold scent bottle which had belonged to some Robertson lady of long ago, or even the horn snuff-box, which just possibly, if not very probably, had been used by James Robertson.

It was in some such way that she had usually comforted Charles in his boyhood, when he had failed an examination, fallen out of a tree or lost a fight, though her gifts then had usually been edible.

Charles's eyes filled with tears. He could hardly bear to look at the big chair where she had sat on the last evening of her life. Getting up restlessly, he turned on the radio and tried to listen to a Beethoven symphony.

That was at ten o'clock.

It was nearly half an hour later that he heard a violent ringing at the door-bell. The violence seemed unnecessary, unless earlier ringing had been drowned by the music, and taking for granted that it was Peggie at the door, he decided to point out to her, as he went to open it, that he wasn't deaf.

But it was not Peggie whom he found at the door. It was Jean Baldrey who stared at him out of the darkness with a white, distorted face and who screamed at him in a high, shaking voice, "Which of you murderers shot my brother?"

# Chapter VIII

DOWN THE dark lane a light shone. As Charles took this in, the picture that had sprung to his mind when he heard Jean Baldrey's words faded. It had been the picture of the farmhouse with the door that had remained closed, although Baldrey's car was standing in front of it. But the light that Charles could see down the lane was the light inside the car, standing in its usual place in the field gateway. Distinct against the darkness behind it were the head and shoulders of a man, slumped over the wheel.

Charles went swiftly past Jean Baldrey to the gate. There he found himself face to face with Ivor, who emerged from the shadow of the chestnuts and moved forward to stand in front of Charles. But it was over Charles's shoulder to the girl that Ivor spoke.

"What's happened, Jean?"

Charles answered, "She says her brother's been shot. You'd better come with us."

In a shaking voice, the girl cried, "You shot him! One of you shot him!"

Ivor pushed past Charles, whom he seemed hardly to see, and thrust a hand through Jean's arm.

"No, Jean! It couldn't have been . . . Wait!" he exclaimed as she tried to wrench her arm away from him. "Wait! You can't know what you're saying."

"I know what I'm saying!" she cried. "Look at that!"

She flung out a hand. It pointed at the

shadow under the trees, near to where Ivor must have been standing a moment before.

Ivor looked towards it in a distracted way, still holding her arm tight, as if he could not make himself let go. It was Charles who followed the line of the pointing finger and in the light streaming out from the door, saw a rifle lying among the daffodils by the gate. He thought that he recognised the rifle. It was one that he had often shot with himself.

"Ivor, isn't that yours?" he said.

Ivor let go of Jean Baldrey's arm and came to Charles's side. The girl immediately went running down the lane. Ivor was going to bend and pick up the rifle when Charles pulled him back. They looked at one another in silence, then Ivor gave a nod, swung round, looking all about him as if he expected to see someone besides themselves in the shadows, then started after Jean. Charles followed him.

Before they had caught up with her another figure, which Charles in consternation took to be that of a child, moved out from the darkness beyond the car and came a few steps to meet the running girl. But when long arms shot out to stop her going any closer to the car, he saw that it was not a child. It was George Nutting, the dwarfish landlord of the White Lion. As Jean stood still, he turned and clutched at the handle of the nearer door of the car to wrench it open.

Charles caught him by the shoulder and pulled him back. Someone in a calm and steadying voice said that if it were true that Baldrey was dead, none of them should touch anything, and it astonished Charles immediately afterwards to realise that this had been himself. He was looking at Baldrey as he spoke, nausea tightening his throat.

He knew that Baldrey was dead. The bullet, if that was what it was, had gone into his left temple. Blood had trickled down the side of his face. But there was not very much blood and the hole seemed to Charles, in his ignorance, very neat, very small, to have been so deadly.

Standing back, he asked Nutting, "Have you called the police?"

"No, I only just got here," Nutting said. "I happened to look out of the window and saw the light on in the car. It wasn't usual, so I came to see what was up. Jean, you'd better come inside. These gentlemen will stay here and look after things. I'll give you some brandy."

She ignored him. Holding her dark coat closely round her she moved away from the men to the middle of the road and stood looking up and down it, as if she were already expecting the police to appear. Her face showed chalk-white in the light from the car.

"I'll wait here till the police come," she said.

Charles was compelling himself to look steadily at the dead man in the car. Something that he had noticed was trying to force itself on his attention and he felt that a moment before he had known quite clearly what it was, yet now his mind seemed blocked. It felt like looking at a familiar face and being unable to fit a name to it.

"Why don't you go in, Miss Baldrey?" he said.

"No," she answered.

"Oh, please, Jean," Ivor said. "There's no point in your staying here. Come in with me and telephone the police yourself. It'll be best if you do it, since you found him. And I'll telephone Deborah. She'll be wondering where I've got to."

"Then go and telephone her," Jean said tonelessly. "And the police, while you're about it."

Suddenly Charles remembered what he had been unable to think of the moment before. "The light . . . Did you find the light on in the car when you came out, Miss Baldrey?"

"No," she said.

"The point is, whoever shot your brother had to be able to see him," Charles said. "Are you sure the light wasn't on?"

The police, he knew, would require her to be sure.

She glanced towards him and he felt piercingly the pain and anger in her eyes.

"Perhaps it was on," she said.

"I wonder why," Charles said. "He usually waited here in the dark, didn't he?"

"Probably it was dark, then. Yes, it was dark."

Ivor clutched his hair. "Can't you even remember whether or not you reached into the car and turned the light on, Jean?"

George Nutting began to speak in a high, chattering voice. "You're bullying her! Leave her alone! Can't you see she's in a state of shock? She doesn't remember anything. How could she? She came out here and found her brother dead. It isn't your business to ask questions. Lights! How

151

could she remember about a thing like lights?"

"I'll talk to the police when they get here," Jean answered. "Go and call them, George."

"I wish you'd come too, Jean," he said. "You need a drink. It'll steady you. You'll feel better."

"Go!" she suddenly shouted at him.

He turned and went hurrying back to the inn at a shambling trot.

She walked a few steps after him, not to follow him, but to put more distance between herself and Charles and Ivor.

Nutting soon returned, accompanied by Professor Stacey. Silently at first, the five of them waited there until the police arrived. Then Ivor made an attempt to talk to Jean Baldrey, but she only gave him a hard stare. When he went nearer to her and muttered something that the others could not hear, she moved away from him. He gave up then and a few minutes later, low-voiced, asked Charles where Peggie was.

"Thank God, she's in London," Charles answered.

"What the hell's she doing there?" Ivor demanded. Shock or anxiety was showing in him as bad temper. He seemed to have forgotten his desire to telephone to Deborah.

"I believe she's checking Baldrey's statement about the value of the things he found in the attic," Charles said.

"She didn't say anything to me about doing that," Ivor said.

"When did you see her?"

Ivor, in his distraction, seemed unable to remember.

"At lunch," he said after a moment. "Yes, that was it. But she didn't say anything about going to London."

Remembering his encounter with Peggie at the gate, and thinking that she might have spared him some annoyance then by telling him that she was going to have lunch with the Heydons, Charles said, "She didn't make up her mind to go until early this evening."

"She's well out of this, at all events," Ivor said. "She's a better shot than any of us, and that gun . . ."

"Well?" Charles said as he stopped.

"Well, she's often used it, she knew where it was. So you're right—thank God she's in London!"

"I've often used it, I knew where it was," Charles said. "And the same happens to be

153

true of you and Deborah and probably a number of other people. Why d'you keep directing suspicion at Peggie, Ivor?"

"*Directing* suspicion?" Ivor said wildly. "That's the last thing I'm trying to do. I'm scared, that's all. Dead scared."

"But why for Peggie?"

"Not for Peggie. Not for anyone in particular. Just for all of us. You were right, weren't you, Charles? Mrs. Robertson was murdered."

Charles nodded. "I should think even the police will agree about that now," he said.

"And Baldrey's been killed, because he knew who did it."

"That's how it looks, though there might be other reasons."

"I think it's a good enough reason. And my gun was used for the job. So I, or someone who knew Deborah and me fairly intimately, did both murders. D'you wonder I'm scared? I suppose you think I'm the murderer, Charles. And that's what the police are probably going to think, isn't it? After all, I'm someone who can always use a little extra money, and if there was something of value in that attic that I stole last night, it all becomes clear as day, doesn't it? And I was out in the road this evening."

"Did you hear the shot?" Charles asked.

He saw a shudder run through Ivor's heavy body.

"No," Ivor said. "Did you?"

"No. But I was listening to the *Eroica*, which isn't the quietest piece of music in the world."

"I hope you'll be able to prove that to the satisfaction of the man with the Plasticine face," Ivor said ironically. "A musical alibi might be over his head. You might do better not to have an alibi at all, like me. Just say you were sitting there quietly, minding your own business, and thought you heard a car back-fire."

"Only I didn't."

"But it sounds better than the *Eroica*," Ivor said. "He'll never believe the *Eroica*— any more than he'll believe my story of how the gun got into the murderer's hands. You know how I think that happened? Deborah took the children out shopping in the afternoon and I went to my room to work, and there I was, typing away, when I heard someone in the sitting-room. Naturally I thought it was Deborah come back for something she'd forgotten—her money or some odd thing like that. So I never thought of getting up to see who was prowling about in our house. And then a little later Deborah came back and I asked her what she'd forgotten and she said she hadn't forgotten anything and hadn't been back earlier. And I thought that was just a harmless little lie, because she doesn't really like being reminded of how forgetful she is and what a bloody muddle she makes of everything. So I never thought of looking round to see if anything was missing—least of all, a thing like a gun. But now, of course, I'm quite sure that that was when it was stolen." Ivor gave Charles a sidelong look. "Well, what d'you think of that, Charles? How do you think it sounds?"

"I think it sounds as if you were making it up as you went along," Charles said, annoyed by the way Ivor had spoken of Deborah.

"That's interesting," Ivor said, "because it's all true. Where were you, incidentally, about three o'clock this afternoon? Because that's when I heard our prowler."

"I was writing a letter," Charles said.

"Writing letters—listening to music. You're sunk, chum—you're absolutely sunk."

With relief, because his temper was beginning to get a little out of hand, Charles saw the police car swing round the corner from the main road.

But Charles knew that Ivor's story of how the rifle had disappeared might be perfectly true. There was a perverse streak in Ivor which sometimes made him mix fact and fiction in such a way as purposely to create doubt and confusion in the mind of his hearer. This was not really in order to delude him, but merely to hold him at bay, to prevent his attacking where Ivor felt himself to be vulnerable.

Inspector Long sent them all into the White Lion, telling them that he would follow them and take their statements shortly. In the room with the horse-brasses and pewter, Charles again found himself sitting next to Stacey on one of the hard wooden settles. Jean had gone to sit in a corner by herself, but Ivor had followed her, had sat down beside her and again started talking to her.

He was incapable of being silent for more than a few minutes at a time, Charles thought. He always had to find someone to listen to him. Except, perhaps, at home. Charles remembered Ivor's sullen silence in his own sitting-room the evening before, and all of a sudden a new and uncomfortable thought came to Charles's mind. Had Ivor stopped bothering to talk to Deborah? Were long and sullen silences common in that house? Was Deborah, as an audience, no longer good enough for him?

Uneasily Charles realised now that Ivor's dark eyes were fixed on Jean Baldrey's face with a concentration which Charles was not the only person to notice. She was making almost no response to his swift, quiet speech, but was sitting rigidly and looking straight before her. Yet from across the room George Nutting, leaning his hunched shoulders against the bar, was watching them both with eyes full of anxious spite. The small man looked as if he could hardly stop himself rushing across the room to separate them.

"Pardon me," Stacey said in Charles's ear. "I hate to intrude my private concerns at such a time, but have you by any chance spoken to Dr. Robertson yet concerning what I told you this morning?"

Charles looked at him blankly. He had just remembered something that Deborah had said to him the night before. She had said that Ivor's drinking was not serious. Charles had not believed her, because it had been so evident that something was wrong in the Heydon home, but now he began to

158

wonder if what Deborah had said had perhaps been the literal truth. Was it not Ivor's drinking that mattered to her seriously, but only where he did it, and with whom?

"The letters," Stacey said apologetically. "Maybe if Mrs. Stacey were here, she'd manage to keep me quiet about them. But without her at my side, I'm not strong enough to resist saying what's most on my mind. Have you asked Dr. Robertson if I may commence a search for the Robertson letters?"

"Yes, and as a matter of fact . . ." Charles felt somewhat ashamed of what he had to say. "As a matter of fact, we had a search for them ourselves this afternoon—without any success. But, of course, that doesn't mean they aren't there. And now my cousin's gone to London. But I think she'll be back to-morrow. Would you care to come up to the house then and discuss the whole thing with her yourself?"

The lines of Stacey's plump face had hardened at the information that a search had taken place without him. After a slight hesitation he said, "Thank you, I'll do that." Then he turned away from Charles and stared thoughtfully at a row of pewter tankards. After another pause, he added,

"This man Baldrey, he's the guy who was in the habit of exploring Mrs. Robertson's attic, isn't he?"

"Yes," Charles said.

"And maybe got my first telegram."

"It's possible."

"Well, well," Stacey said and started to chew the tip of a thumb. He kept himself silently occupied with this until Long and the sergeant came into the room.

The questioning that followed took place in George Nutting's small office. Jean Baldrey went first. As the door closed behind her, Ivor joined Charles and Stacey at their table. Charles turned to Nutting, meaning to invite him to join them too, but Nutting took care not to notice this and went out quickly through the door behind the bar.

Ivor ruffled up his fuzz of hair and gave a loud, resentful groan.

"Someone ought to do something about that girl," he said. "I've been trying to, but she won't listen to me. I think she's got me ticketed as First Murderer. All the same, I don't think she ought to go back to that farmhouse to-night. I've told her we can give her a room and we'd be glad to have her, but she only stares into space and says no, she's going home. Well, I can't stop her,

160

but I don't like it. I wouldn't do it myself in her place. Not for anything."

Charles's suspicions of Ivor's interest in the girl immediately seemed to him extremely shabby, and with a sort of bewilderment he wondered what it was that really had made him feel them. Had it been something in Ivor, or something in Jean, or had it been simply the sharp, jealous gaze of George Nutting?

Stacey was saying, "If there's difficulty about a room for her, Mr. Heydon, she's welcome to mine here, and I'll find another in some other hotel. If I can't get a taxi to take me there at this time of night, maybe Mr. Robertson would drive me over."

"If it came to that, you could come to us," Ivor said, "but I'm afraid Jean wouldn't stay here either, because Nutting's a bit of a problem for her. That was the real reason why Baldrey always came to meet her. If he didn't, Nutting always tried to see her home. He's not at all a bad little man, but Jean had more than enough of him in the daytime, and it didn't help that he and Baldrey detested each other—a sort of jealousy, I suppose. Baldrey was furious about her working here, and showed it by refusing to wait for her in front of the pub itself. He may have taken her working as a criticism of him, because he'd never settle down to a proper job. If it was, it's about the only one she ever made. She was a damn promising actress, but she gave it all up to come here and keep house for him." Ivor frowned down at the table, as if he were wondering suddenly why there was no drink upon it. "Pity, for his own sake, when you come to think of it, that Baldrey had that kink," he added, "because I don't suppose he'd have got shot right in front of the pub. Not from our end of the lane, anyway. You can't see into the car park here from up there."

"To a determined murderer," Stacey said, "the precise location may not always be a decisive factor."

"Anyway, how did the murderer see him, even in the gateway," Charles said, "if the light wasn't on in the car?"

"Obviously it *was* on," Ivor said. "Jean just got muddled about that."

"But how did the murderer know it was going to be on?" Charles asked.

"I'm just thinking aloud," Stacey said, "and it occurs to me that the dead man might have been sufficiently illuminated for the purposes of the murderer by the headlights of another car, approaching from this direction. A figure in silhouette against a strong light would make an admirable target."

Ivor slapped the table and his features lit up with enthusiasm. "I believe you've got something, Professor! But wouldn't it be too chancy? There's very little traffic down this lane at any time, and practically none at night. Or could it have been conspiracy? Two people, I mean, one to drive the car and one to shoot? Only why do it like that? It seems so complicated. There'd be far simpler ways of shooting a man."

"Just a minute," Charles said. "It might not have been chancy at all. There's one time when anyone who knows the neighbourhood at all could count on lights shining down the lane."

"Yes, yes—the bus, the bus!" Ivor shouted. He slapped the table again and his face shone with relief. "Baldrey was shot when the last bus turned the corner by the pond. And we know the time of the last bus. It gets here at ten-twenty. And I've got an alibi for ten-twenty. I've got a perfect alibi. I was here till closing time, then I walked home and by ten-ten at the latest I was at home with Deborah. She'll swear to that, and that I didn't leave the house again until just a minute or two before ten-thirty, when Jean came running down the lane and started banging on your door, Charles. Even if my gun was stolen for the job, and even if they work it out that I've a hundred motives, it doesn't matter at all because I've got an alibi!"

The loudness of Ivor's voice had brought Nutting back to the door through which he had disappeared a few minutes before. With a shoulder against the doorpost and his head only just showing above the bar, he stared at Ivor with sardonic contempt. Charles was wondering for perhaps the thousandth time what Deborah had ever been able to see in someone so childishly egotistical. It must be the very childishness, he thought, that worked upon her, the utter simplicity of Ivor's concentration on himself.

"Was Baldrey already in the gateway when you left here at closing time?" Charles asked him.

Ivor turned to Nutting. "George, can't we have drinks all round?" he said. "We need it."

"What, after hours and with the police in the house?" Nutting said with obvious

164

satisfaction at being able to refuse. "I'm surprised at you, Mr. Heydon."

"Aren't the circumstances exceptional?" Ivor said pleadingly. "Wouldn't the police overlook it for once?"

"When they can't drink themselves, because they're on duty? I'll serve Mr. Stacey, as he's staying in this hotel, but not anyone else," Nutting said.

"No, thank you—no," Stacey said quickly. "It appears to me advisable to retain what clearness of mind I am capable of."

"Ivor, was Baldrey already in the gateway when you left here at ten o'clock?" Charles repeated.

"I don't know," Ivor said fretfully, scanning the rows of bottles behind the shelves, as if he were considering helping himself. "I suppose so."

"Can't you remember?" Charles asked.

"No, not really," Ivor said. "One got so used to his being there, one didn't think about it. But it doesn't signify, does it, so long as he was there before the bus came along? That was a brilliant idea of yours, Charles, about the bus. I wonder if the Plasticine man has got on to it yet."

"You aren't the only one it gives an alibi

165

to, Mr. Heydon," Nutting said, "if what a man's wife is ready to say ever counts as an alibi. Jean didn't leave here until nearly half-past ten. She and I were in here together cleaning up, so that lets her and me out."

Charles thought of asking Stacey where he had been at that time. Had he been in the White Lion, and if so, had he heard or seen Jean Baldrey and George Nutting, busy at their clearing up? But as Charles was turning this over in his mind, the sergeant came in and told him that the inspector would like to speak to him.

For the next half-hour, watching Long's expressionless face, with the eyes that seemed incapable of showing shock, anger or distress, Charles was able to think of nothing but certain statements made to him by Long. These were that Charles had no shadow of an alibi for the murder of David Baldrey, that he had been where he might have heard the shot, that Beethoven was not the best possible excuse for having failed to do so, and that he had had a better opportunity than anyone else for the murder of Mrs. Robertson.

"So you've changed your mind about

that, have you?" Charles said. "You've decided it was murder."

Long's eyes evaded Charles's for a moment, and something that might have been anger made a muscle twitch in his cheek.

"There's rather more evidence than there was before," he said, "unless someone's used the accidental death of Mrs. Robertson to confuse us about the real motive for killing Baldrey. But if Baldrey was killed because he knew too much about the death of Mrs. Robertson, then it's a reasonable conclusion that you were right and that I was wrong. Now, please tell me, Mr. Robertson, what do you know about some valuable papers which Miss Baldrey says she heard you and Professor Stacey discussing this morning?"

# Chapter IX

WHEN CHARLES was allowed to go, he intended to go straight back to the house to see if Peggie had returned. If she had not, he intended to telephone her flat, to tell her of the murder of Baldrey, and also that the police intended to search the house for the love-letters of James Robertson.

Charles found something so fantastic in the thought of that search that even in his anxious and exhausted state, he felt a wry sort of mirth stirring within him. He thought of Long's big, blunt hands fumbling with the precious pages, and his unshockable gaze travelling over the faded, difficult script in which an obscure young man of long ago had recorded his passion, never dreaming that all the time he had history peeping over his shoulder, in the person of a police inspector.

The picture of the two of them together, James Robertson in his wig and bottle-green coat, and Inspector Long in the felt hat and raincoat which he wore like a uniform, seemed to Charles so preposterous that he had an uncomfortable feeling that he was going to burst out laughing at any moment. The fact that he felt that he might not be able to control the laughter, that it might bellow out of him in helpless hysteria, made him hurry from the White Lion, grim-faced, to find himself, just outside the door, face to face with Jean Baldrey.

She looked very tired, very haggard and very unsure of herself. She seemed to want to say something, yet not be certain if she dared. The fury that had sustained her earlier had burnt itself out. Now there were only exhaustion and misery.

Charles asked her, "Have they said you can go?"

"Yes," she said.

"But you can't possibly go back to your home," he said. "You'd be all alone there."

"That's all I want," she answered, "to go home and be alone."

"Do you really mean that? Wouldn't you sooner go to some friends?"

"I'm not sure if I have any friends here."

She still stood in front of him, blocking his way and with that uncertain, waiting look remaining on her face, so that Charles felt that he would have to ask the right question for her to be able to say to him what she wanted.

"If you don't mind waiting here for a few minutes," he said, "I'll get my car and drive you home."

"It isn't far to walk," she said. "I think I'd sooner walk."

"Shall I walk with you, then?"

Something about her relaxed, as if she had gained what she wanted.

Wondering at it, because it seemed to him that it should have been easy for her to ask him to see her home, Charles stepped through the doorway. She turned as he did so and took a few steps, not in the direction that he had expected, but towards the village.

"Isn't that the long way round?" he asked.

"There's a short-cut through the wood," she said.

He remembered then that about half-way back to the main road there was a stile from which a path ran through a wood to the Baldrey farmhouse. He and the girl walked towards the stile in silence. When they had climbed it, Jean went ahead, her feet dragging on the damp carpet of leaves. Again Charles had the feeling that there was something which she was waiting for him to say, but this time it was beyond him to guess what it was.

It was very dark under the trees. At moments Charles might almost have thought that he had lost her if it had not been for the rustling of the leaves at her feet.

Presently she said, " 'Life without friends means death without witnesses.' "

Charles started. "What was that?"

She repeated it, adding, "I forget who said it. There's truth in it, isn't there? David hadn't any friends."

"If someone's made up his mind to kill you," Charles answered, "he'll find a time when there aren't any witnesses, even if you've got all the friends in the world."

"But you know what I mean," she said.

"Yes, I suppose I do."

"He made friends easily. People always took to him at first. But he couldn't keep them. And he never could understand that. The only person who stuck to him was Mrs. Robertson."

"What about you?" Charles said.

He heard her draw a shaky breath. "Perhaps I shouldn't have stuck much longer. You can take on things that are too much for you."

"What made you take it on in the first place?"

"It was when he came out of gaol," she said. "It seemed the only thing to do."

"Gaol?"

She appeared not to hear the surprise in the word, and to take it for granted that Charles knew what she was talking about.

"He'd have gone to pieces completely if I hadn't," she said defensively, as if he had criticised her for what she had done. "But it was a mistake coming back here. The house was empty, so it seemed the easiest

171

thing to do, and we didn't think many people knew about his sentence. All the same, I ought to have remembered that it's the people who've always known you who'll never give you a chance to change. They've made up their minds about you and they don't want you to be different. So we ought to have sold the farm and started again somewhere new. Only I suppose something of the same sort would have happened wherever we'd gone. One can't really change. One can try awfully hard, but sooner or later one's own nature always gets the upper hand."

"Wait a minute," Charles said. "Before you go any further, I ought to tell you that I'd never heard anything about his having been in gaol. I don't know what he'd done, or what sentence he got for it."

She stood still, looking round at him. Charles stood still too. His eyes had grown accustomed to the darkness and it seemed to him that the expression on her white face was rather scornful.

"I can hardly believe that," she said.

"Why not? Who could have told me?"

"Didn't he tell you himself?"

"Except when we were both children, I'd never met him till yesterday. Was it something he told to people as soon as he met them?"

She considered the question, then shook her head. "But didn't Mrs. Robertson tell you?"

"No."

She drew another shaky breath. "She was good, that old woman. David got six months for obtaining money on false pretences. It was from another old woman. He sold a lot of pictures and valuable old china and so on for her, and then managed to hang on to most of the money."

She turned as she spoke and walked on again.

Following her, Charles said, "I suppose what you meant when you said that one's own nature always gets the upper hand in the end, is that you think he'd been doing the same again."

"I listened to you and the American," she said. "But I knew before that that something had happened. I mean, before Mrs. Robertson was killed. David was extraordinarily excited and he wouldn't tell me why. He said he'd tell me when he was sure about something. And then when she was killed . . ." She paused for so long that Charles thought that she had changed her mind about going on, but at last she added, "You think he killed Mrs. Robertson, don't you? You've thought that from the first. You think that as soon as he saw you go on down the lane and knew that she was alone, he ran up to the house, stole those letters from the attic, met her on the way down and pushed her down the stairs and killed her."

"Aren't you forgetting," Charles said, "that I'm the person who gave him his alibi?"

"But that's what I can't understand," she said. "You must have known it was I you'd seen in the car when you came back from posting the letter. You couldn't possibly have mistaken me for David. We aren't at all alike. Yet you told the police it was David you'd seen."

This time it was Charles who stood still. She walked on, unaware of it, and after a minute he went hurrying after her.

"Are you telling me the truth?" he said. "Was it you in the car when I walked back?"

"You know it was."

"I don't. And I don't think I believe it. I don't think you even expect me to believe it."

"But it's the truth."

174

He caught her by the shoulder and swung her round to face him.

"Listen, if I knew it was you in the car, and yet told the police it was your brother, that'd mean that I was his accomplice in the theft of the manuscript and the murder. And that makes me probably his murderer too. And if you really believed that, you wouldn't have asked me to walk home with you through this dark wood."

"If anything happened to me, they'd know it was you," she said. "George Nutting watched us walk away together."

Charles turned that over in his mind, tried to see himself with her eyes as a possible thief and murderer, but found it beyond him. He gave a shake of his head. "I don't think you really believe it. So why did you say it?—that's the question."

He saw the gleam of tears on her lashes.

"Well, why, *why* did you say it was David in the car? He told me you had, and said since you'd done it without being asked, there was no point in telling the police the truth, as sticking to your story would save a lot of trouble. But then they found his fingerprints on the switch and knew he must have been up there sometime that evening and that probably you and he were lying about his having been in the car—and it hasn't saved trouble, it's made trouble. So if you weren't in the thing together, why did you do it?"

"Believe it or not, because I really thought it was David in the car," Charles said. "I suppose it's just possible that it wasn't. I remember the bus had just gone by and everything immediately afterwards seemed very dark. And I didn't want to stop again and have another talk, so I didn't look very carefully at the car. I just waved at him and he waved back—that is, I thought it was he who waved back. I never even thought of its not being your brother. Now tell me why you really asked me to walk home with you."

With an odd mimicry of his way of talking, she said, "Believe it or not, because I'm afraid of the dark."

She set off again along the path to the house.

She walked fast now until they reached the point where the path joined the drive about twenty yards from the house. From there Charles saw the dark bulk of the building with only its doorway lit up by a light shining through the glass panel in the door, just as it had been earlier, when Charles had come to see Baldrey. Jean was breathless now, and stopping in the soft, sodden grass at the edge of the drive, caught Charles's arm.

"Look," she said, "we always leave that light on because I can't bear coming home to a dark house. It's stupid to be afraid of the dark, isn't it? But it's what I am. So thank you for seeing me home. Good night."

She shot away from him down the drive towards the house.

It took Charles by surprise and he almost did as it seemed she wished, which was to turn and start walking back by the way that they had come. But he did not think that he and Jean Baldrey had said all that they had to say to one another, and by the time that her key was in the lock, he had caught up with her.

"I don't think you expect me to believe much of that either," he said.

"Oh, you think you know too much about what I expect—altogether too much," she said. She threw the door open. "Well, come in if you want to."

She went in herself, switching on more lights as she went.

Charles saw the stone-flagged hall that he

remembered, the steep stairs, and through an open door on the left, the big kitchen. It had been the kind of kitchen that dominates a house, giving it a core of cheerfulness and comfort. As Jean led him into it, he saw to his surprise that this was still what it was, a bright room, all fresh paint, polished flagstones, gay china and shining copper, and with a welcoming feeling of warmth that came from a big, old-fashioned range. There were none of the usual signs of defeat, the dust and the drab air of neglect.

Jean saw Charles's surprise and said in a colourless voice, "You can't argue the point, David was a wonderful housekeeper." She went to the sink and filled an electric kettle. "If you'll come in and sit down, I'll give you some coffee."

"Is this all David's doing?" Charles asked.

"Most of it," she said. "He liked pottering about a house, redecorating and mending things—only sometimes he'd stop in the middle, because he'd thought of something else he'd like to do. But on the whole it's what he did more methodically than anything else. He was a born odd-job man. A wonderful odd-job man." In spite of her effort to keep it neutral, her voice started to shake again.

Charles sat down at the big table in the middle of the kitchen. It was an old wooden table, with its top scrubbed white.

"I still can't understand," he said, lighting a cigarette. "You don't speak of your brother as if you thought he was a murderer, and if you really thought I was one, I don't think you'd have brought me home with you."

"There you go again," she said. "But with your wonderful insight into my mind, where's your difficulty? Just tell me what I think and I'll agree with you."

"I don't think you think your brother killed my aunt."

"Oh, you're right, you're right!"

"Am I?" Charles asked evenly.

"Indeed you are—that was agreed in advance."

"Please!"

She slowly put down a milk bottle which she had just emptied into a saucepan. She turned to look at him curiously.

"I did think you faked that alibi on purpose," she said.

"But why?"

"I don't know. People can have such

complicated reasons for telling lies, reasons no one else can understand. Living with David, one couldn't help finding that out."

"I wish you'd tell me more about David—what he was really like, I mean."

"Do you really?"

"Wouldn't you like to? Mightn't it help?"

She stood quite still for a moment, tense, as if a tone of sympathy were the last thing that she had been expecting, and something that she hardly knew how to cope with. Then she said, "All right. If that's what you want. Though I'm not sure if I can do it. It's something I've never tried to do before. Sometimes I've thought about it so much that it's become a sort of obsession, but I've never tried to talk about it to anyone else."

"Try now, then," Charles said.

"Well, then," she said, "he was a crook. He was a liar and a thief. And he was kind, gentle and generous. And he happened to be the person I've cared for all my life more than anyone else."

She looked Charles in the eyes as she said it, then sank on to a chair at the table, dropped her arms across it and her head on to her arms and let the tears come.

Charles finished making the coffee. He brought it to her and made her drink it.

When, after a time, the tears stopped, the words came in a swift, smooth torrent, a flood that had broken the dam that had held them back. Charles thought that at times she did not know to whom she was talking, and that if he had wanted to stop her, he could not have done so.

She told him of her brother's arrest, never suggesting that there could be the faintest doubt of his guilt. She added that he had been in trouble before, but had always been lucky enough to be forgiven—or unlucky enough, she said, because getting away with things wasn't always the most fortunate thing that could happen to you. And David had always been able to get away with things, because there was the side of him that was gentle and sweet, and which wasn't put on, but was perfectly genuine, perhaps more genuine than the other side of him, which didn't mind fading out of the life of a trusting friend with five hundred pounds or so that had somehow been left in his care.

When that happened, Jean said, it would never have been planned in advance. It would be the sudden decision of desperation, because the five hundred pounds, or the fifty, or the five, would somehow have melted through his hands before he was even aware of it. And heaven only knew where the money went, because he wasn't really extravagant. He wasn't a heavy smoker, he drank very little, didn't travel, didn't give a thought to his clothes, and though a woman who was kind to David could do almost anything she liked with him, he had never really become entangled with one. Perhaps books were his only serious extravagance, and reading, wide, disconnected reading, his only vice.

After the arrest had come the trial and the sentence. Jean paused at this point, her gaze fixed on empty space, as she relived an experience that she did not intend to describe. She said only that she had attended the trial, and then had visited David in prison. In prison he had made a great many good resolutions. He had said that the big mistake of his life had been trying to escape from the world where he belonged and that what he had to do now was to go back to it and pick up his life where the war had broken it off.

"He even talked about going back to the land," Jean said, "but that I never believed in. You can't suddenly turn yourself into a farmer just because it sounds a good idea— not when you've already resisted it all your life. Besides, he was the sort of person who likes quick results and lots of variety. But, as I told you, the house was here and I thought if I came too and we stuck together, we could work something out. He was a good mechanic and carpenter and so on, and if only he'd stuck to that . . . But that was always the trouble, he couldn't stick at anything. And the people here didn't help us —except Mrs. Robertson. She used to ask David over to do all her odd jobs and used to keep him on, talking to her, taking an interest in all the odd things he was interested in, giving him the run of her house and treating him like an ordinary human being. But she never pretended he hadn't been in prison, or let him pretend it, either. And David loved her. That's what you've got to understand."

Charles slipped in his first question. "How did she find out he'd been in prison?"

"I made him tell her when she started being so good to him," Jean said. "And because of the way she took it, he worshipped the ground she walked on. When she had her fall and couldn't walk, he was over there for hours every day, carrying her about as soon as that was possible, and looking after her. Then a few weeks ago he found those things in the attic. . . ."

Jean sighed and leant back in her chair.

"You see, that in itself was a bad sign, though I didn't realise it at the time, because he wouldn't have found them if he hadn't been poking about. He told me about the books and the picture and told me he'd told Mrs. Robertson. I . . . As a matter of fact, I rang her up and made sure that he had told her and she said that he had and I'd nothing to worry about. And I wasn't really worrying, because David had never simply *stolen* anything, and I knew that if Mrs. Robertson trusted him, she was doing it with her eyes open. But pretty soon afterwards I began to worry, because I began to feel there was something that David hadn't told me. He was sort of excited. You could see he had something on his mind that he was awfully pleased about, and he made one or two trips to London and wouldn't tell me what they were for. I think now they were probably to the British Museum, or wherever he could check up the handwriting of those letters. But all he'd say was that I was to wait and he might have something terrific to tell me soon. Then suddenly he'd go depressed and say it was probably all a mistake and the trouble was he'd never had any real education or training and couldn't trust his own judgment. And then Mrs. Robertson was killed."

Jean was speaking quite calmly now. Putting her elbows on the table, she looked directly at Charles, instead of into the dark shadows of her own mind.

"I'll tell you what happened that night. I mean, I'll tell you what I know 'of my own knowledge.' Isn't that the phrase? I came out of the pub as usual at about a quarter past ten. The car was there but David wasn't. I got in and waited. Then you went past and you waved to me, which surprised me rather, because I didn't know you, but I thought you were probably someone who'd been in the pub sometime and recognised me. And two or three minutes later David came running down the road, jumped into the car and drove off like a madman. His face was white and he was shaking and he wouldn't turn on the car lights. He nearly ditched us in the pond. And at first he wouldn't say anything at all. I don't think he could have said anything, his teeth were chattering so. I had to give him some brandy before he could start to tell me what had happened. Then he told

185

me that just after you'd gone by, he'd seen a light flickering in one of your attic windows. He said it looked as if someone was using a torch up there. So he'd gone off to investigate, because he knew you'd just gone out and so Mrs. Robertson was almost certainly alone in the house and she couldn't possibly be up in the attic. Well, you know what he found. Mrs. Robertson was on the stairs, just as you found her. But David thought he heard a sound at the back and he might have gone to see who it was, only he thought Mrs. Robertson moved then, so he ran to her. But she was dead. So then he ran up to the attic."

Jean paused again, frowning.

"That was something I couldn't understand at the time. Why, if he'd heard a sound at the back, did he go straight up to the attic? He couldn't explain it. He said it was where he'd seen the light and that he hadn't been sure about the noise. But when I heard you and the American talking, I realised what had happened. He'd gone straight up to the attic to see if the Robertson letters were safe—the letters he wasn't sure about, not absolutely sure, and so hadn't said anything about to Mrs. Robertson. You may think that was because, if they

186

were what he thought they were, he was going to steal them. On the other hand, perhaps he was thinking of them as a wonderful return that he could make to Mrs. Robertson for all her kindness. That's what I really think when I don't suddenly have awful doubts about him. I think they were to be the grand gesture that was to put everything right for him. But of course the papers were gone."

"Do you think he knew who'd taken them?" Charles asked.

"Of course," Jean said.

"Of course?" Charles almost shouted it. "But then he knew who the murderer was!"

"I think so."

"And you mean you didn't realise it?"

"I only realised that he'd gone clean distracted. But I thought it was because of his grief, mixed up with the fear that if it was murder, he'd be suspected. And now I think that besides all that, he was trying to make up his mind what to do. He was never very good at making up his mind and in the end usually acted on some crazy impulse."

"But if you're right that he knew—or thought he knew—who took the papers, it could only be because he'd told someone about them."

"Yes, I know. And that would have been just like him. He was never much good at keeping anything to himself. That was partly why it was so easy to convict him that other time."

"Yet he kept it from you."

"And from Mrs. Robertson, because it was to be a wonderful surprise for us both to find out how clever and how honest he could be. But that doesn't mean he didn't chatter to a dozen other people."

"But you said he had no friends."

"No."

"Are you sure?"

"Yes."

All at once he doubted her. He did not think that she was at all sure. Her answer had come too decidedly, while her eyes regarded him a little too steadily.

"You think you know who it was," he said. "Don't you?"

She shook her head.

Her drawn features worked on him like a plea for mercy, but he went on, "Tell me who it was, Jean. The person you seem to be protecting killed your brother."

"No, she didn't."

"She?"

"Of course, he'd only confide in a woman."

"Who was it?"

"She couldn't have killed him. Whoever killed him was a very good shot. That's what that man Long said. And she isn't. Besides, she—she's had rather a lot to bear lately, and—well, I don't want to make things worse for her than they are already. And . . ." She gave her head a quick shake. "I'm not even sure about it. It's only that a couple of times in the last month I've found cigarette-ends with lipstick in the ash-tray in the car. There were a good many of them, as if she'd been with him for quite a long time. The first time I asked David whom he was getting off with and he said it was just some girl he'd given a lift to. But then it happened again, and, you see, it was the same lipstick as before. And they were his cigarettes, the kind he nearly always smokes, with cork tips. That's all." She stood up abruptly. "Now would you mind leaving, because I'm very tired. It was kind of you to come, and this talking has helped a lot, and I think I'll get some sleep now."

He did not move. "What colour was the lipstick?"

"But she couldn't have killed him. Even if he talked to her—"

*"What colour was the lipstick?"*

She gave a little shrug of her shoulders. "Pink," she said. "A bright sort of pink. And there was rather a lot of it, as if she'd put on a lot too much."

Charles's heart was beating and his hands felt cold.

"You're telling me," he said, "that you think it was Mrs. Heydon."

# Chapter X

AS SOON as the words were out, hot fury engulfed Charles. He had been feeling sorry for the girl, had been admiring her loyalty to her brother, had felt moved by the way that she had spoken of Mrs. Robertson, had been thinking her honest and generous and had believed almost everything that she had said. But now all that he could think of was that she was a trained actress, and that her true reason for asking him to walk home with her had become abundantly clear. It had been so that she could make him say the very words that he had just spoken.

The jealous, hungry way that George

Nutting had watched her and Ivor in the bar came back to Charles then. Jean had stared straight before her. She had pretended not to be listening to what Ivor had been quietly whispering. She had acted an angry suspicion of him to perfection. But then she had brought Charles home with her and hesitantly, reluctantly, making him wring the story out of her, had told him that Ivor's wife had been in the habit of meeting David Baldrey secretly, and was the one person to whom he might have told the secret of the James Robertson letters.

Disgust choked Charles. Usually anger released a flood of speech in him, making him overstate his own feelings with a sort of reckless enjoyment. But now he was dumb, scared for once of what might happen next if even the first word of rage came out.

After a moment he stood up. He was meaning to walk straight out of the house without speaking again, but Jean, who had been watching him with something dying in her face as she did so, and something else, a scornfulness, almost a look of mockery, such as he had seen there in the wood, taking its place, lifted her head and said coldly, "I *said* she couldn't have killed David."

Charles paused on his way to the door.

"You said it, but did you want me to believe it?"

"You know all my thoughts," she said. "Work it out for yourself."

"I'll give you something to work out," he said. "She's rather short-sighted. You may not have realised that, because she hardly ever wears glasses. But whatever suspicions of her you try to work up, *she could not have fired that shot!*"

"I think that's just what I told you," Jean said. "But if David could talk, so could she—perhaps to some old friend she hadn't seen for a long time."

Her glance challenged him to answer her. Charles turned on his heel and went out.

He walked away fast through the wood. His anger was singing in his ears and his lips moved swiftly as he silently told the close-growing trees, the trailing brambles and the unresponding shadows what he might have stayed to tell the girl if, for that minute or two, he had not become frightened of his own rage.

He wondered if she had already told her story to the police. Or Ivor's story. It was perhaps more likely to have been Ivor's production than hers, Ivor who had sat whispering his instructions into her ear, and then, a few minutes later, had led the conversation in the pub to his own cunning alibi.

But it was unimportant which of them had planned the crime. They were in it together, and in the midst of Charles's chaotic thoughts, he saw with a deadly clarity what the next step would be. The old story of Charles's love for Deborah would be raked up. When next Charles met Inspector Long, it would turn out that he had been informed of it. And after that the letters, or rather, a few of the letters would be found where only Charles or Deborah could have hidden them. Both would be arrested and some time later the rest of the letters would be secretly sold to some unscrupulous collector, and Ivor, rid of his too loving wife and Jean of a burdensome brother, would marry and live affluently ever after.

Yet somebody had made a mistake. Something had been said that evening that should not have been said, that spoiled the pattern. Charles was aware of this even though he was both thinking and walking too fast to be able to say, for the moment, where the error lay. It was only when he reached the road and saw the house ahead of him, its windows lit up and police cars in front of it, and knew that the search for the letters was proceeding, that he became sufficiently conscious of his surroundings to stand still and consider what he ought to do next, and in that pause saw, all at once, what had been eluding him.

Jean had warned him. Whether she had let it slip out accidentally because she was angry at her failure to make him think as she wanted, or whether she had had some more complicated reason for saying what she had, the fact was that by telling him of David's supposed intimacy with Deborah, and pointing out that Deborah might then have talked to another friend, she had warned Charles of the danger to both of them.

He knew what he wanted to do now. Reaching the main road, he turned to the left and went to the Heydons' house. Ivor opened the door when he rang and gave a great yawn in Charles's face.

"I thought you'd be along, somehow," he said thickly. "God, I'm tired! Aren't you tired? You look as fresh as a daisy. What a thing it is to be strong and healthy. Was I ever strong and healthy? Do I remember what it was like not to ache in the joints and to use the nights for sleeping? You know, Charles, it's an extraordinary thing, but I can't honestly say I do. Can't honestly say I remember, I mean. I know that once upon a time there was a man called Ivor Heydon who slept at night and didn't ache in the joints, but I can't remember what it was like to be that man any more than I can remember being an infant in arms. You can remember having been ill when you're well, but you can't remember having been well when you're ill. I'm horribly ill, Charles. I'm sick with misery and self-pity. Come in and help me drown the blasted things."

Yawning again, he went to the sitting-room, leaving Charles to follow him.

In the sitting-room Ivor threw himself full length on a sofa, closed his eyes and let one arm trail limply on the floor, as if he were drunk or asleep. But he went on talking.

"How long before they arrest me, Charles? I'm the murderer, did you know that? I took my own gun and strolled out of your gate, waited till some headlights lit me up nicely for all to see, took a pot-shot at poor old Baldrey, dropped the gun among the pretty flowers and strolled home. Couldn't be simpler, couldn't be more obvious. But what a fool I must be! Would you have thought I was that much of a fool, Charles? Would you, now? Tell me honestly. Don't mind my feelings."

"Frankly, I shouldn't have thought you were, Ivor." It annoyed Charles that it had been Ivor who had opened the door to him, because he had nothing to say to Ivor until after he had spoken to Deborah. "But if the murderer stood among the chestnuts, the bus driver wouldn't have seen him."

"Frankly—he said frankly," Ivor muttered. "That's what people say when they don't mean what they're going to say. Frankly, candidly, to tell the truth, old chap . . . After that there's a lie coming." He opened his eyes, but kept his bleary gaze on the ceiling. "Why didn't you remind me of my alibi?"

"I didn't think it was necessary," Charles said. "Has something gone wrong with it?"

"One car too many, that's what's gone wrong," Ivor said. "Haven't you seen the man with the Plasticine face?"

"Not since I left the pub."

"You haven't been in next door?"

"No. I took Jean Baldrey home, then I came straight here."

Ivor moved his head slightly to take a swift glance at Charles. "Then you don't know if Peggie's got back yet?"

"No."

Ivor gave a sigh, closed his eyes again and seemed to forget that he had been about to say something.

Looking down at him, Charles thought that his face had the grey, soiled look of a handkerchief that has stayed too long in a pocket. His collar was unbuttoned and the ends of his tie hung loose over a stained pullover.

"Has Long been here?" Charles asked.

"Yes, he and his familiar spirit, the silent sergeant," Ivor answered. "What a life that sergeant must lead, Charles. Can you imagine it—walking about on his two feet, listening, and who knows, even thinking, but never opening his mouth? Could you do that? I couldn't. It'd be the death of me."

Because the tension in him was mounting with his impatience, Charles's voice became louder. "Why did Long come here?"

"To tell us about the extra car, and incidentally give Deborah a fit of hysterics. She knows I murdered Baldrey now. And of course I murdered Mrs. Robertson too, to get my hands on some priceless letters which—isn't it odd?—I haven't the faintest idea how to sell now that I've got them. So they must be around somewhere. Just take a look, Charles. Perhaps you'll turn them up somewhere, then we can go fifty-fifty on the proceeds. We'll both be rich—if you know who buys things like that on the quiet without swindling one out of half their value. I don't like being swindled. After I've gone to all the trouble of committing two murders to get them, I shouldn't like to be swindled, Charles."

"The car, Ivor—the extra car!" Charles was almost shouting. "What do you mean by an extra car?"

"A car that came down the lane a few minutes before the bus," Ivor said. "A car which—would you believe it?—stopped at the corner by the duck pond and shone its lights down the lane. And then vanished."

"Who saw it?"

"A man called Dainton, who lives in that cottage beyond the White Lion—the one that's been modernised. He was out in his garden, meaning to go and meet the bus, because his wife had been up to London, and was going to catch the last bus back from the station. A devoted husband, you understand. The bus-stop is only three minutes' walk away from the Daintons' gate, but he went to meet her. And being about seventy-five and a bit slow on his feet, he gave himself plenty of time to get to the bus stop. So he was walking down his garden path when he saw this car stop by the pond."

"What make of car?" Charles asked.

Ivor gave an ironic snort of laughter. "Don't be an ass, Charles. Nothing in life is as simple as that. The Daintons don't own a car. They never have owned a car. They are very nearly the only people in the whole country who have never wanted to own a car. The old man can no more tell you what make of car that was than he can fly."

Charles sat down and lit a cigarette. "Wasn't it Baldrey's car?"

"That's what I said to Long," Ivor answered. "I said, 'I'm not sure about it, but you can check up with the couple of people I walked home with—I mean, that Baldrey's car wasn't in the usual place yet when we went by. And if it wasn't, it had to get there somehow, and after we'd turned the corner too, or we'd have seen the lights from behind us. So wasn't it simply Baldrey's car the old man saw?' But it seems Dainton saw the driver and swears it was a woman, with a scarf knotted under her chin. He didn't see her face and wouldn't recognise her, but he won't be shifted on the point that she was a woman. And so it immediately became obvious to Deborah that this woman was someone I was in cahoots with to do the murder, and she started to have hysterics." Ivor thrust thick fingers through his hair. "Thank God the children slept through it all. You can usually count on them to do the opposite of what you want, but this once they managed to do the right thing, bless them! What a night!"

Charles had not been taking Ivor's fears for himself very seriously, thinking that they were merely part of the masquerade, yet he thought that he had heard an undertone of real anxiety in Ivor's voice when he spoke of Deborah's suspicions.

"Is that really all this man Dainton saw?" Charles asked.

"Well, no," Ivor said. "There was another detail. He says that when the car stopped, the woman stuck her hand out of the window to signal that she was stopping."

"In a dark country lane, with no traffic behind her?"

"That's what he says."

"Well, I suppose she might."

"That's what Long said. He didn't seem to think it important. My own feeling, you know, is that anything that man says is important you can safely forget about on the spot, and anything he says is unimportant will turn out to be the thing that solves the case."

Charles was frowning. "What seems to me important about that piece of information is that it couldn't be true."

"Oh, you needn't doubt Dainton. I know him. The old boy's eminently honest," Ivor said. "Sane, too, except about not wanting a car. I'd like to have a car, Charles. If I'd stolen those letters successfully, I'd go straight out and buy a car. A splashy job, too. Showy. I like a showy car."

"All the same, if he was in his garden, which is on the right side of the lane, and a car came along the lane in this direction, and the driver made a traffic signal of any sort, it would have been on the side of the car away from his garden, wouldn't it? And in that case, he couldn't have seen it."

Ivor sat up abruptly. He brought his feet

to the ground with a thump. The bleary look had gone from his eyes.

"You're sharp as a needle, Charles," he said. "Forgive me if I say I'd never have expected it of you. You're dead right. Dainton couldn't possibly have seen that signal at all, *unless the car had a left-hand drive!*"

"Yes," Charles said, "unless it was a foreign car."

"And if it was a foreign car, it's got nothing to do with the case!" Ivor slapped his knees, laughed, and a look of the deepest relief appeared on his face.

Deborah heard the laughter from the doorway. In a horrified tone she exclaimed, "Oh, Ivor!"

Charles stood up and took a quick step towards her. But she did not look at him. She was white and haggard and her eyes were red from the tears which were still damp on her cheeks. Her hair hung limply about her face. She looked as if she were so exhausted that she could hardly stand.

Holding on to a chair to steady herself, she said, "That laughing—it was horrible. And you'll wake the children. And just look at you, you need a shave, your hair looks as if you haven't combed it since the day

202

before yesterday, your shirt's filthy. I don't know what's the matter with you."

Ivor gave her a strange, malicious smile. "I'm a murderer, darling. I've forfeited my right to belong to the human race. So why worry about a few refinements?"

"But it doesn't help," she said. "We've got to pull ourselves together. Both of us. We've got to start helping each other a little."

Ivor swore under his breath and walked out of the room.

Deborah dropped into a chair as if she had been thrown there. Then her hand crept out for a cigarette and thrust it between her bright pink lips. But she seemed unable to bring the tip of the cigarette into the lighter that Charles held out to her. As the cigarette wavered, she drew little gasping breaths and seemed surprised and irritated that it would not light.

Charles steadied it with a hand under hers. This was what he had come for, to see her alone and tell her of what perhaps menaced them both. But he doubted if, in the state that she was in, she would even be able to listen if he tried to talk.

He gave her a moment of quiet, then said,

"Ivor's just been telling me about the car that came along the lane before the bus."

A muscle twitched beside her mouth. She did not answer.

"Is it true, Deborah, that Ivor got home before the bus came along?"

She nodded, still without speaking.

"But only just before, is that it?" Charles said. "So that if there was a car a little earlier, he might have shot Baldrey against its lights—that's what you're afraid happened, isn't it?"

"Yes," she said hoarsely.

"Only you don't know that it was probably a foreign car," Charles said. "Does that mean anything to you?"

She gave him an intensely startled look. "A *foreign* car?"

"Yes, and Ivor was laughing with relief because he said that meant it couldn't have anything to do with the case."

"A foreign car," she repeated wonderingly. "How do they know that? Who saw it?"

"That man who lives in the cottage beyond the White Lion. He said he saw a traffic signal, which he could only have seen if it had been made on the left side of the car, which means a car with a left-hand drive, and that's almost the same as saying a foreign car."

"Then—then it probably *hadn't* anything to do with the murder at all." She gave a strange, radiant smile. "What a fool I've been, haven't I? I always behave like a fool. No wonder Ivor was so angry—because I did suspect him, of course. It was his own fault though. Ever since he got back this evening he's talked so queerly that he drove me nearly out of my mind. And he kept telling me about his alibi with the bus, as if he thought I might forget it. And I thought I knew who'd been driving the car . . ." She stopped, flung her cigarette into the fire and clapped both hands over her mouth.

Charles sat down near her and spoke gently. "Who did you think it might have been?"

"Oh, Charles, please——!" Her voice went high and shrill. "Don't question me. I didn't mean that. I didn't really mean anything."

"Was it——?" he began, but she interrupted him. "No, no, no, don't go on about it. It doesn't help to talk about it. I can't, I won't!"

There was such frenzy in her voice that

Charles decided that to talk of it just then might actually be dangerous for her.

He patted her shoulder and stood up. "All right, Deborah, I won't ask you any more. I'll go home."

"No, don't go," she said quickly and caught at his hand. "We could talk about something else, couldn't we? I'd like you to stay and talk about something else. Anything. Anything ordinary."

"I don't think I *could* talk about anything ordinary," Charles said.

"Couldn't you try? I need it. I need it terribly, Charles. It's so long since I've had anyone to talk to about anything ordinary.

"But, Deborah——" Pity and a fearful sense of helplessness overcame him. He sat down again. She went on looking at him as if she expected him to go on and, after a moment, feeling foolish and entirely inadequate, he said, "Well, tell me something about the children. What are they doing?"

"Oh, they're asleep, thank heaven," she answered eagerly. "They must have worn themselves out with excitement, because they're both sleeping like angels, which isn't at all like them when there are people coming and going. It's awful, isn't it, but in a way I believe they've been enjoying it all—

not understanding, of course, not really understanding anything. They don't really see the difference between what's happened and their games of cowboys and Indians. They look at Inspector Long as if her were a sheriff from the Wild West . . . Oh, there I go!" Her voice went soaring up again. "One can't keep off it. You're right, it's no use trying."

Charles had practically forgotten what he had come for in the intensity of his feeling that Deborah had to be comforted at any cost.

"Listen," he said, "I know you're almost mad with fear that Ivor did the murders. But that doesn't really make sense unless you haven't told the truth about the time that he got home. If you have told the truth—and you and Ivor are the only people who know if you have or not—then you really haven't anything to worry about. Whoever shot Baldrey had to be able to see him, and if Ivor wanted to murder him, he'd hardly stroll out there with his own gun, on the off-chance that some lights would shine down the lane at a convenient time, then afterwards drop the gun among the daffodils, where it was bound to be found at once. So unless you can somehow tie him up with that foreign car——"

"I can't," she interrupted. "That car can't have anything to do with the case."

Charles was surprised at how convinced he felt by his own argument for Ivor's innocence. He had been in too much of a hurry on his walk back from the farm to work out just what steps Ivor must have taken if he had killed Baldrey, but describing them now, it almost seemed to Charles that he would have to abandon the suspicions that had driven him headlong from Jean Baldrey's presence.

"I wonder," he said thoughtfully, "if Baldrey was really sitting there in the dark. If, for some reason that we don't know anything about, he'd arranged to turn on the light inside the car, he'd have made a sitting target. After all, we've only Jean Baldrey's word for it that she found him in the dark as usual. If in reality it was she who turned the light off before she came for me——"

"Charles, stop!" Deborah turned towards him and hammered at him with her fists. "Ivor didn't do it. You've just proved that yourself. And if the light had been on in the car, Mr. Dainton would have seen it when he went to meet the bus. So don't start it all over again. Try to think of who else could have done it, if you want to, but forget about

208

Ivor. Why should you think it could have been Ivor?"

"Why did you?"

"Oh, that was different. That wasn't—wasn't real. I knew all the time that he wasn't capable of murder. It was just that —oh, I believe you know it, so I may as well say it. I've lost my old feeling of trust in him because he's lost his love for me."

Charles immediately wanted to deny it, to reassure her, to tell her that this could not possibly be so. Yet with her admission, there had been a slight relaxing of her features, and after a moment she even managed a forlorn smile.

"Oh, I think everyone knows it," she said, as if he had actually uttered his contradiction, "so why should I pretend? And it's really a relief to have said it, though I'd never have thought it could be. I've had a sort of feeling all this time that if I never said anything about it, it couldn't be true. Silly, wasn't it? I've always been silly about all sorts of things, which I suppose is why Ivor's got tired of me. But he loves the children as much as ever, so I've thought that if I could stand it, he'd come back to me in the end. In a way, you see, that's what he wants himself. He'd love to have back the

209

old easy days when we all loved each other and he had an easy conscience. And this may sound absurd to you, Charles dear, but it's his conscience I'm really afraid of just now. It's been tearing him to pieces. It's been driving him mad. He thinks about the children and that, whatever happens, he's got to provide for them and me, and so he hates me and he drinks to drown his hatred and he can't sleep. Sometimes he *is* almost mad, Charles. And so am I. I've had no one—no one at all—to talk to about it, not even Mrs. Robertson, whom I used to be able to talk to about anything. Once or twice I tried to, but she couldn't bear it and she headed me off, and then I felt worse than before I'd tried."

"And ever since she was murdered, you've been suspecting Ivor of having done it to get the Robertson letters, so that he'd be able to provide for you and the children and go off and leave you with a clear conscience—is that it?"

"I didn't know anything about the Robertson letters until Ivor told me this evening, when he got in from the pub, and said he'd heard about them from Inspector Long," she answered. "But I knew, of course, that some old books and things had

210

been found, and I thought perhaps they were really more valuable than people thought they were."

This was the point when Charles could have told her that the police would probably shortly be suggesting to her that she had known of the existence of the Robertson letters for considerably longer than she had just said, and asking her when she had last gone for a drive with David Baldrey. But he thought that if he questioned her directly on whether or not there was any truth for the police to work on in Jean Baldrey's statement that Deborah and Baldrey had known each other better than either had ever admitted, he would meet only frenzied denial. She had just carefully told him that Ivor had first heard of the letters after Baldrey's murder, and she would see the danger to Ivor in saying anything that might suggest that he could possibly have obtained knowledge of the letters earlier through her.

Until now Charles had not asked himself seriously if there could be any truth in Jean Baldrey's allegation. But feeling the continuing fear in Deborah, and remembering her fit of hysteria when Long had told her of the car that had been seen by the old man in the cottage, information which for the moment had destroyed her faith in the alibi that she was able to give Ivor, Charles began to wonder if it might not be credible that she had been in Baldrey's confidence. For months she must have been in a state of lonely desperation, and Baldrey, with his odd, gentle charm, might have given her a little help and comfort.

"For some reason," Charles said carefully, "you're still rather afraid, aren't you, Deborah? But now that we've disposed of that foreign car, and since you yourself know that Ivor was at home when Baldrey was probably killed, there's really no reason for you to be afraid, is there?"

"I'm afraid people aren't going to believe me when I say Ivor was at home when the bus went by," she said. "Even you aren't absolutely sure if you believe me about that, are you? You know I'd lie or do anything else to help him whenever he wanted me to. But he *was* at home then, Charles—I solemnly swear it."

"What brought him out again after it?" Charles asked.

She raised her hands a little, opening them with the palms upwards, as if she was yielding something up to him.

"He was hoping to see her, of course,"

she said. "That's when he often saw her. He'd spend the evening in the pub, because he couldn't bear spending it at home with me, then he'd wait for her there, by the gate, and then they'd go for a walk together. That was their idea of discretion, a country walk in the dark." She gave a short, bitter laugh.

"I don't understand," Charles said. "I thought Baldrey always drove her home. I thought that was why he waited there."

She looked bewildered. "Baldrey?"

"Yes. The story—though I admit it's Ivor's story—is that if Baldrey didn't fetch her, George Nutting took her home and she didn't like that."

"Took whom?" she asked.

"Jean Baldrey."

"Jean Baldrey!" Deborah's voice shot up again in thin, wild, angry mockery. "Is that what you've been thinking all this time? My God, what a fool you are, Charles! Ivor's never given that girl a thought. It's Peggie he's in love with—your cousin Peggie!"

# Chapter XI

THE POLICE had gone when Charles returned to the house next door. There was

213

no sign of Peggie. In a mood of sullen rage with himself, Charles went up to his room, threw off his clothes, left them where they fell and got into bed. His head was aching and his eyes were burning. When he tried to close them, the lids flew up again as if they were on springs, letting the darkness press its evil weight on his eyeballs.

He could not even begin to sort out all the blunders that he had made, but the one that filled him with the most disgust was the way that he had behaved to Jean Baldrey. The girl had asked him to walk home with her probably for no other reason than the one that she had given him, that she was afraid of the dark. If perhaps she had also thought it expedient to impress on him the fact that it was she and not her brother whom he had seen on his return from the letter box, that was a natural enough thing for her to have done, for it had been merely reclaiming from her brother the alibi that could no longer serve him. But then she had confided in Charles, letting him understand a little of the tragedy of both loving and understanding a man like David Baldrey, and she had wept in front of him, which he did not think was the sort of thing that she would ever do easily. And Charles's response to it all had been practically to accuse her of being an accessory to her brother's murder and of trying to cast suspicion on Deborah and himself.

His anger with himself made him scowl and lash out at the darkness in front of him with a clenched fist. How could anyone have been as blind as he had been, as blind and cruel? He was always going off half-cocked, seeing what he took to be the truth in white-hot flashes of what he mistook for intelligence. In fact, he thought, he was dull-witted and insensitive. And having these appalling defects of character, how could he really expect a woman like Sarah Inglis to make up her mind to marry him? When he got back to Edinburgh, wouldn't he find that she had changed her mind, had weighed him and found him wanting? An appalling anxiety crept up on him out of the silence and chill of the night.

He slept at last and awoke late. The day was like the day before, grey and gusty, with raindrops slithering down the window panes. When he went downstairs he found Peggie at breakfast in the dining-room. She had left her black dress behind in London and was wearing a grey flannel skirt and cashmere jumper. With her pallor, the shadows round her eyes and her grey hair, she looked at least ten years older than her age.

"When did you get back?" Charles asked as he sat down and poured out a cup of coffee.

She answered listlessly, "About half an hour ago. I needn't have gone. I took the portrait out of its frame, but there wasn't anything there at all, and I took that volume of the Proceedings to a man I know, who specialises in things like that, and he says that if the run's complete for the thirty years, it's worth about ten pounds a volume. So Baldrey told the truth about that, as far as it went. Then I felt too tired to drive down here again, so I went to a cinema, and when I got back to the flat afterwards, I found the police waiting for me, wanting to know where I'd been. And it seems that, unless I can prove I was at the cinema, I might just possibly be a woman who drove a car along the lane and stopped by the duck pond at about ten-ten, shining my headlights on to Baldrey, while you or Ivor shot him. Or I might have shot him myself when the bus came along the road. Altogether an unfortunate evening."

"I don't think you've got to worry about

216

the risk of being taken for the woman in the car," Charles said. "It was almost certainly a foreign car, and so nothing to do with the case. All the same, it would probably be useful if you could prove you were in the cinema."

"I shouldn't think I can," Peggie said. "I didn't pay for my seat with a five-pound note, I didn't stamp on anyone's feet, I didn't drop my cigarette ends down any-one's back, and the film was an old one, anyway, so having a vague memory of the plot doesn't help." She got up from the table and went to look out of the window. "But unless someone can prove I'd a motive for killing Granny, they won't be able to find I'd any for killing poor David."

"He's become poor David, has he?" Charles said. "What's changed your mind about him?"

"It hasn't changed," she said. "It's just that death makes most things seem trivial, particularly one's own likes and dislikes. And I suppose because he can't injure me any more, I feel I can afford to be sorry for him. I always was rather sorry for him, ac-tually. He'd all sorts of nice qualities, mixed up in the mess."

"How did he injure you, Peggie?"

She leant her forehead against the glass of the window pane and did not answer.

After a moment Charles said, "I had a long talk with Deborah yesterday evening."

"Oh?" she said.

"I've been a blind sort of idiot, haven't I?"

"Well . . ." She paused, then she turned round and came back to the table. She poured some more coffee into her cup, drank it and said, "Yes, Charles, you haven't been bright. David was much brighter than you. He was the first person who found out about it. That was because I told him. And he told Deborah. That's what he did to me."

"How do you know he did? Did Deborah herself tell you so?"

"Oh, no, we don't speak. We aren't civilised types. It's war to the knife between us."

"If you don't speak, how did you manage to have lunch with the Heydons yesterday?" Charles asked.

"I didn't," Peggie answered.

"Ivor said you did."

She gave a sardonic laugh. "Another gratuitous alibi, or something, that he forgot to mention. What a hell of a husband the man would be. When men tell lies, they ought always to prime their womenfolk beforehand, so that we can back them up with becoming loyalty. I had lunch with Ivor at a pub on the river. I was waiting for him at the gate when you came back from your talk with Professor Stacey."

And it had been Ivor, Charles thought, whom Peggie, earlier that day, had run to the door to meet, only to find David Baldrey on the doorstep. Her rage with Baldrey had probably been three-quarters disappointment.

"You haven't said yet why you think it was Baldrey who told Deborah about you and Ivor," he said. He tried to make his next question sound casual. "Did they know each other as well as all that?"

"I didn't think so, or I'd never have talked to him in the way I did," Peggie said. "But only a couple of days after I'd told David all about us, Deborah told Ivor that she knew he and I were in love with one another."

"Couldn't she have got there on her own, just by knowing the two of you?"

"I suppose so, only I don't think she did. And when I accused David of it, he didn't deny it, he only looked hang-dog and miserable."

"Anyway, whom did that really harm?"

"That's quite a question, isn't it? I know you're on Deborah's side in this, Charles. How could you help it? She's good and sweet and wronged. I'm almost on her side myself, and so is Ivor, naturally. So perhaps what I was really angry with David about was finding out that even he wasn't on my side, although we'd sat there so long and so late, talking so intimately and trustingly when Granny was ill. That's when it all began, you know—when Granny had her accident."

"I don't think I'm really on anyone's side," Charles said. "Not at present. I'm too damned confused and I've been making too many mistakes about everybody."

"You never were very clear in the head," Peggie said. "And nor is Ivor, particularly when he's frightened."

"That sounds very dispassionate for a woman in love."

"What chance have I had to be anything but dispassionate?" she asked with sudden violence. "I've had an awful lot of time just to sit and think about him, getting to know him in my own mind with quite dreadful clarity. I could tell you every single thing that's wrong with that man, beginning with his utter inability to make up his mind about anything, or take any real responsibility. If he could do either, he'd have left Deborah months ago, or else decided to see no more of me. And whichever he decided, it'd be better for both of us, but by now he's got us both on his poor old conscience and so he's stuck with us."

"Wouldn't it be possible to take the responsibility yourself?" Charles asked. "I shouldn't have thought it's a thing you'd ever be afraid of."

"You mean cut my own losses and hand him back to Deborah, all safe and sound? I said you were on her side, didn't I?"

"I've at least a lot of prejudices in her favour," he admitted.

"Of course you have. But to give him back is the only decision I can take by myself, because I can't make him leave her, however hard I try. I can only decide to do the leaving. And, believe it or not, that's just what I've tried to do over and over again. I tried putting an end to everything, and even got you to come down here to try to persuade Granny to move up to London, because as long as she was here, I'd have to keep on coming back, and whenever he thought I was back, Ivor always rang up and then it would start again. I'm not at all strong-minded when I'm actually near him. If he wants me, I just go to him. Seeing him turns into the only thing in my whole world that matters, though if you ask me *why* . . . But I don't suppose you'd be as foolish as that. There's never a why, is there?"

"So when he rang up just after I'd found Aunt Alice," Charles said, "saying he'd seen lights and was wondering if anything was wrong, it was really because he thought you might have come down."

"Yes, of course," Peggie said. "I told you it all began when Granny had her accident, didn't I? You see, for the first months I came down every week-end, and for as much of the vacation as I could, and Ivor and Deborah were being very kind and neighbourly to her, so of course I saw far more of them than I ever had before. Then the children got measles—Harriet had it rather badly—and Deborah couldn't get out much. You remember how the two of them used to do almost everything together? Well, Ivor didn't much enjoy going about on his own, so I started to go with him. We used to go shooting . . ."

Her hand went to her mouth. For an instant stark terror looked out of her eyes. Then, as if Charles had spoken, she said furiously, "All right, I'm a good shot and so's he. And even Deborah knows how to fire that rifle and that goes for you too. But what's that got to do with it? Would any one of us, after doing the murder, have dropped the rifle there by the gate?"

"I've been worrying about that," Charles said, "and I can think of only two possible reasons for doing it. One is that the murderer was surprised and had to get rid of it sooner than he'd intended. The other is that it was a clumsy attempt to incriminate you or me."

"But you've still got to find a motive for any of us to have killed Granny. Just find a motive!" Peggie cried. "Say we all knew something about the Robertson letters—we didn't, but say we did. And say we wanted money badly. I don't know about you, but it's certainly true of me. Money for Deborah and the children would have done half the job of calming Ivor's conscience. Well, as I told you yesterday, if those letters had turned up while Granny was alive, she'd simply have handed them over to me. The difficulty would have been to make her keep them. You agreed about that."

"Yes," Charles said, "I did."

"And Ivor knew it as well as you do, and that if I'd got them that'd be almost the same as if he'd got them himself. And Deborah, to be fair all round and give her her due, has as little interest in money as anyone I've ever met. She's quite content to muddle along on the edge of poverty, as long as she's got Ivor and the children."

"Yes."

"So that leaves only you with a possible motive, and you see I'm generous enough not to suggest you've got one."

"Thank you. All the same . . ."

Charles had been trying to remember something that had been said to him recently, which he had an unreasoning conviction was relevant to this conversation. It was something to do with money, but who had said it, or when, or where, he could not recall. He had a feeling that it had been said in a masculine voice, and while Peggie argued, her swift flow of words confusing him, he had been trying to go over the conversations that he had had with Ivor, with Stacey, with Long, to see if he could somehow startle the hidden memory into show-

224

ing itself. But except from Stacey, who had talked vaguely of gold, oil and uranium, Charles thought that he had heard surprisingly little about money.

Then all of a sudden, almost as if the words had been spoken aloud in the room, he heard Baldrey's voice.

"What about death duties?" Baldrey had said, sitting in the car in the darkness of the lane.

Charles gave a little start and Peggie noticed it.

"What's the matter? Have you thought of a motive for yourself after all?" she asked.

"Perhaps we've all got one," he muttered, drinking the rest of his coffee quickly and getting to his feet. "I've just remembered there's someone I've got to telephone," he added and went out.

From Directory Inquiries he obtained the private number of a solicitor friend of his in London. He was someone whom Charles had not seen for about five years, and the friend spent several minutes of the call asking what country Charles was ringing up from, when Charles was next going to be in London, and when they were going to go fishing again together. Charles said that they had never been fishing together, and the friend said that that might be so and that he was probably mixing him up with somebody else, but that all the same it was very pleasant to hear from him. After that he agreed to listen to Charles's question.

As Charles put it, it was a hypothetical question, concerning what might have to be paid if papers of some value were discovered in a house where they had stayed hidden for several generations, passing with the house and its contents from one owner to the next. The friend said, "Hum," whistled a bar of music and said, "Ha," then said that this was a very difficult thing to answer, because the answer in law was often quite different from the answer in practice, and anyway, there was a period of twenty years laid down beyond which no fresh claims could be made.

"So if nobody's died for twenty years, there's really nothing much to worry about," the friend said. "Why don't you take up fishing, Charles? We could see more of each other."

"But if three people have died?" Charles asked.

"Well, that's rather different. You'd probably have to pay the amount appropriate to the value of the estate as a whole at the time of each death. It's all extremely complicated. I can't really tell you anything unless you tell me a bit more about what this mysterious undisclosed asset is, and what it's worth, and so on. Then I'll do my best to work it out for you and write you a letter."

"I'm not even sure there is any undisclosed asset at all," Charles said.

"Well, you're paying for the call, old boy. Anything else I can tell you?"

Charles said that it looked as if there wasn't and rang off. He was left with a not very distinct impression that since his father had once owned the house and its contents, had left it to his younger brother George, who had made it his home for all the years that the elder brother had been in Africa, and since George had left it in turn to his wife Alice, and since all these three had died within the last twenty years, a not inconsiderable proportion of the gold, oil or uranium that Professor Stacey had hoped to discover would have passed out of Peggie's hands if she had waited to inherit the papers legally from her grandmother. And even if her grandmother had given them to her as soon as they were found, Peggie might still, at a later date, have had to pay the same duty as she would have had to pay if she had waited to inherit them, since Alice Robertson might not have lived long enough after making the gift for it to have been exempt from taxation.

So whatever Peggie might say about her own certainty that her grandmother would have given her the valuable letters, it seemed to Charles that it was not possible to say that Peggie could have had no motive for stealing them. And if Peggie had a motive, Ivor had a motive. And since her mind was far quicker than Charles's, she probably knew all this, having arrived there long before him.

When he returned to the dining-room, he found Peggie still there, standing by the window, looking out at the garden. Her face was as bleak as the grey sky. Charles went to stand beside her. Remembering his crassness with Jean Baldrey, he found that the more reasons for suspicion of Peggie that he was able to discover, the more doubtful of himself he became, and the more ashamed. Yet the suspicions would not leave him. He did not know what to do with them, whether to keep them entirely to himself, to tell her about them, or to tell Long.

No, not Long, he thought, not that man.

This was Peggie, whom he had known all her life. Or never known at all, of course. That was another way of putting it.

He was hesitating when Peggie began to speak.

"There are some things, aren't there, which you never take entirely seriously, even if they're the most serious things in your life?" she said. "I mean, however much you plot and plan, you never honestly believe they'll happen. There's always a dream quality about them, just because they matter to you so much. I don't think I've ever really believed Ivor would leave Deborah and live with me. There was just a short time at the very beginning when I thought I couldn't lose, but that passed very quickly and since then I've really always accepted defeat. I've kept up the struggle, because it felt less awful than giving in completely. All the same, that's what I've got to do now, isn't it? I've got to sell this house and keep away. And I'm a very lucky person, really. I've got what's called a future ahead of me. Oh, yes, I have—I don't need any monument to be patient on. I can go back to work and enjoy it. Only . . . Only I do wonder what would have happened if we'd been able to raise some money."

"Peggie—look at that car!"

Charles barked it at her so that her last few words were lost. He thrust her to one side, flung up the heavy window, jumped out and went running down the drive.

But he was too late to stop a very long and wide American car, driven by a small woman in a flowery hat, passing the gate and turning down the lane towards the White Lion.

# Chapter XII

CHARLES SAW the car stop at the White Lion. By that time he was walking fast down the lane. After a moment he heard Peggie's footsteps behind him, and he paused a moment to let her catch up. She had not understood his excitement and was annoyed with him because he had interrupted her confidences.

He explained, "I told you the car that came down the lane at ten-ten and stopped beside the pond was probably a foreign car. And so, I said, it had nothing to do with the case. Which shows how easy it is to forget a great big obvious fact like the fact that Professor Stacey told me he'd brought his car to England and that his wife had it with her in Stratford on Avon."

"That's Mrs. Stacey?"

"Who else could it be? And she isn't in Stratford on Avon, and she and her husband have quite as much to do with this case as any of the rest of us."

"The police didn't say anything to me about its having been a foreign car when they questioned me last night," Peggie said. "They only talked about a car driven by a woman with a scarf tied over her head."

"Didn't they tell you she made her traffic signals on the side of the car that Dainton, the man who lives in that cottage down there, could see from his garden?"

"They may have. I wasn't thinking much about the car itself, but only about that cinema I'd been to, and whether or not there was anyone who might remember having seen me there. So you think the Staceys are our murderers?"

Charles stood still. He realised that this was just what he had been thinking for the last minute or two, but hearing it suggested in Peggie's clear, positive voice made him recognise that yet again he had leapt straight to a conclusion, instead of reasoning his way there.

"Who knows? Perhaps they just couldn't bear to be parted any longer," he said as he walked on again. "Or perhaps Shakespeare was a disappointment."

"But the police didn't know anything about her turning up here last night, did they?"

"I don't think so."

"And why did she happen to stop just at that corner by the pond, at just that time?"

"Oh, I agree, it's very suspicious," Charles said. "But it's going a little fast to say they're murderers."

"You may remember I've been suspicious of him from the first," Peggie said.

"All right, but don't start the conversation with them now by telling them so," he said. "A reason why she stopped her car might be that she saw something happen in the lane that we'd all like to know about. In fact, she may simply be by far the most important witness in the case."

"I shan't say anything, I'll leave it all to you," Peggie said.

This was more than Charles could believe. Peggie expected to control any situation in which she was involved. If he had known any way of inducing her to go home, instead of going on with him to meet the

Staceys, he would have urged it, but in fact there was too little hope of it for him to waste effort on persuasion.

They found the Staceys embracing with little excited cries of gladness and relief in the doorway of the White Lion.

"I knew you'd come, honey," Stacey was saying delightedly. "I knew I could count on you."

"Why, of course, Harlan," his wife answered. "It's wonderful to know you needed me. Besides, everything shuts in Stratford on Avon on a Sunday at this time of year. The season hasn't begun yet."

She was a small, plump woman of about the same age as her husband. Her grey hair was faintly blued and curled prettily under her flowery hat. She wore a tweed suit and a short fur jacket. Her face was round, with soft, pink cheeks, a wide, cheerful mouth, a buttonlike nose and blue eyes that expressed a calm, innocent self-assurance.

Her husband introduced Peggie and Charles and she greeted them gravely, with a word of sympathy to each for their loss. But behind the gravity some excitement bubbled.

"I can hardly believe I'm really seeing two Robertsons in the flesh," she said. "I've heard so much about you, I've felt you all belong in a story-book. It's wonderful to see you're really just like other people."

"I think she's sometimes wondered if I didn't invent you," Stacey said. "I ought to tell you, maybe, that she's typed out all the manuscript of my book—so that's the story-book she's referring to."

"The book that's to be finished before we go back home," she said. "That book's been part of our lives for twelve years. Yet now he says he's going to finish it in the next six months—can you imagine that? I've said to him often, 'Harlan, don't ever finish that book—you'll be lost without it, you'll become an old man before your time.' I tell you, Dr. Robertson, I'm truly frightened of what will become of us when that book's finished. It'll be like retirement is for some men. They look forward to it all their lives, and when it happens they don't know what to do but die."

"Now, honey, I can always go back right to the beginning and revise it for the second edition," Stacey said. "What do you say we all go indoors now and have a drink? You could use one after your drive, couldn't you?"

"Couldn't I, though!" Mrs. Stacey said

with enthusiasm. "I started at dawn and crawled the whole way at twenty miles an hour. This driving on the left side of the road has put years on me. After this you can do the driving, Harlan, till we get to France."

"You started from Stratford at dawn?" Charles asked.

"Well, at about eight o'clock this morning, Mr. Robertson," Mrs. Stacey answered. "That wasn't exactly at dawn, but it was very early to be up and about on a Sunday morning. But when Harlan telephoned me last night and told me what had happened, I promised I'd get here just as soon as I could." They were filing into the bar, and she broke off to exclaim with admiration at the oak settles and the pewter. Then, as they all sat down, she added, "I'd have come right away, only Harlan was even more nervous of my driving than I was myself, so I promised I wouldn't leave till it was light. And it's taken me all of four hours to get here, so if I'd left at midnight, I mightn't have been very welcome to the management when I arrived. This doesn't look like the kind of place where there'd be a porter to open the door to the chance visitor."

It was very circumstantial. Perhaps too circumstantial. Peggie thought so, Charles realised, as she caught his eye across the table. But for the present she kept her promise not to interfere. Only the tightening of her lips showed how difficult she found it to keep the words back.

Charles noticed also an uneasy look in Stacey's eyes, as if he thought his wife was talking too much. But how was anyone to tell that this look did not normally come there when Mrs. Stacey started talking? And how was anyone to know if she was talking any more than she usually did?

George Nutting came through the door behind the bar and served them. He did it silently and there was enmity on his pale, nervous face. When he had brought the drinks, he disappeared through the door, but left it ajar, and Charles knew that anything said in the bar would be heard in the room beyond.

He did not think that this mattered. He had nothing private to say to the Staceys. In fact, since he had heard Mrs. Stacey's alibi for the evening before, he had nothing much to say to them at all. The person with whom he needed a talk was Inspector Long, in case Long had not yet perceived the significance of the signal seen by Dainton from his garden, followed by the appearance in the village next day of an American car driven by a woman.

Long could question Mrs. Stacey, as Charles could not. He could check her statement that she had been in Stratford the evening before and answered a telephone call from her husband. He could work out whether, if by any chance she was not really as nervous a driver as she said, she could have been beside the duck pond at ten minutes past ten and back in Stratford by midnight.

Charles thought that he himself could drive the distance in two hours, at least if the roads were empty. But it would be a near thing. To guarantee being back in her hotel to answer a telephone call at what would have had to be a prearranged time would have been singularly bold. But she looked a bold little woman.

She was telling them now about the rigours and the rewards of a visit to Stratford on Avon in the early spring. It had been cold, it had been wet, and the theatre season had not yet begun. On the other hand, she had had the place to herself and had been able to spend two hours in the Birth-Place without hearing a single other American voice.

"And I didn't come on my first trip to Europe to spend my time among Americans," she said. "Harlan and I aren't like that. We want to see the way people over here really live. Well, I do—Harlan only wants to see the way Robertsons live. But I guess at bottom you aren't as different from other people as he thinks and, if he studies you, he'll end up knowing as much about things in general as I do."

She gave Charles her sunny smile and he smiled back, but what he was thinking about was the Heydons' rifle. Could Stacey be the person whom Ivor, from his study, had heard come into the house while Deborah was out shopping? Could Stacey have taken the rifle?

It seemed unlikely that he could even have known of its existence.

Yet for two American cars to have become accidentally involved in the case seemed rather too much of a coincidence. The Staceys were in this thing up to the neck, they had to be, for it must have been Mrs. Stacey in the car that Dainton had seen.

Yet Charles could not understand why they should have worked out such a com-

238

plicated and risky way of killing Baldrey. He saw that they could have been in some sort of conspiracy with Baldrey about the letters and needed to kill him afterwards, or he might have seen them when he rushed along to investigate the light in the attic and so needed to be silenced. But Charles could not see why it had been done in the way that it had. Not by the Staceys. And that meant that he had missed something, or misunderstood something. He started, realising that Stacey had just addressed him and that he had no idea what had been said.

But he never found out what Stacey, looking at him with a frown of cold absorption, had said, for at that moment the door was thrown open and Jean Baldrey came running into the room.

As she came swiftly to the table, she looked only at Stacey. She was red-cheeked from running, her hair was windblown and wet with the rain. Out of the pocket of the old coat that she had on over a cotton overall she brought an envelope and put it down on the table in front of Stacey.

"Look at what's in that," she said, "and tell me what they are."

At the first sound of her voice, Nutting appeared at the door behind the bar. He started to speak to her, but then as he saw the way that she and Stacey were looking at one another, his mouth closed.

"Go on!" she said to Stacey. "Go on!"

One of Stacey's plump, pink hands came out hesitantly. He picked up the envelope. But he seemed unable to tear his gaze away from the girl and held the envelope cautiously without looking at it. He seemed to need some other sign from her, or the answer to some question that he had not asked, before he dared to look at what he held.

Mrs. Stacey spoke to him softly, "Go on, Harlan—open it."

He looked at the envelope then. It was a cheap white envelope, and plainly there was nothing much inside it. One or two sheets of paper at the most. With an air of sudden decision, he slit it open and looked inside.

Charles saw his face become very pale. With gentle fingers, Stacey took out of the envelope two small scraps of paper and laid them tenderly on the table before him. They were all that there was in the envelope. Each piece of paper had a few words written on it in faded brown ink and was charred round the edges. Looking at them, Stacey gave a slight shudder and his mouth began to work.

Mrs. Stacey laid a hand on one of his and said, "Yes, they're his, aren't they? You were right. They were here."

"Yes," he said. "That's James Robertson's writing. I'd know it anywhere. Even these few words . . ." He raised his head and looked at Jean Baldrey. "Is this—all?"

"All that's left now," she said.

"The rest were burnt?"

She nodded.

Peggie gave a hoarse exclamation and started to her feet.

"That can't be true!" she cried. "Who'd burn them? What good are they to anyone burnt?"

"They're all burnt," Jean said. "Just those two bits got left. They'd dropped down through the bars somehow and I found them in the ashes underneath. The rest—well, there's some papery sort of ash at the back of the stove, but that's all."

"What stove?" Peggie asked. "Where?"

"Our kitchen stove." Jean looked at Charles. "They must have been smouldering away while you and I were sitting there talking last night. The fire was very low, or I don't suppose anything at all would have been saved. I've only just found them, because I didn't clean out the grate till a little

241

while ago, because the police came this morning and searched the house and I just sat and looked on till they'd finished. They did find something in the dustbin and they questioned and questioned me about it, but I couldn't tell them anything. It was a volume of the Proceedings of the Royal Society, with the inside hollowed out. I suppose it's where the letters were hidden all those years. And they looked into the stove, I remember, but they didn't look in the ashes underneath. I suppose—I suppose they weren't looking for letters that had been burnt, because of course they *aren't* any good to anybody."

Peggie's mouth was hard with rage. "Didn't you burn them yourself? You or your brother. Didn't you get frightened and burn them?"

George Nutting brought both his large hands down on top of the bar with a noise like a shot.

"Don't you ever say anything like that again," he shouted. "I've said it before and I'll say it again, if anyone knows where those letters went to, and how Mrs. Robertson fell downstairs, and how Baldrey got shot, it's you—yes, you or Mr. Heydon—and I'm not going to have you in here, saying wicked things to Miss Baldrey, not while I'm here to look after her. You can take yourself off now. You can get out quick, or I'll call the police."

"Call them," Peggie said. "Call them at once, please. They should certainly know about this discovery."

"Dr. Robertson—Mr. Nutting," Stacey said in a hushed voice.

He had put his elbows on the table and was holding his head in his hands. His whole being was concentrated on the scraps of paper before him. His elbows were defences on either side of them. His chest was a wall under which they were sheltered. Charles was not quite certain, but he thought that there were tears in Stacey's eyes.

As the others fell silent, Stacey went on in a tone so reverent that he might have been in the presence of the dead, as perhaps, in a sense, he felt himself to be. "This moment is both tragic and wonderful. It's tragic, deeply tragic, because of what's been lost, but wonderful too because at least something has been left to us. These two fragments are, in my opinion, without any question in the handwriting of James Robertson. To see them is the most profoundly moving experience of my life, excepting only the discovery that my love for her was returned by Mrs. Stacey, and I feel I may say with certainty that so deep has her understanding always been that she feels not the slightest twinge of jealousy at my mentioning the two experiences in one breath."

The breath had been a long one. He let it out with a soft sigh, and added, "Take a look, will you?"

As Mrs. Stacey said in a shaky voice, "Why, Harlan!" and dabbed at her eyes, Charles and Peggie looked over Stacey's shoulders.

He barely moved to give them a clear view of the pieces of paper. It might have been distrust of them, or sheer inability to detach himself any farther from the precious fragments. Charles, stooping over the table, felt a good deal of admiration for him. To be able to find satisfaction in this small result and to dwell on it rather than on the shock and disappointment of learning that the rest of the letters were burnt, was dignified and courageous.

To Charles himself the writing on the scraps of paper meant very little. There were only a few words on each and they were in the unfamiliar script of another century.

After a moment he said, "I'm afraid I can't make much of it."

Peggie said nothing. Her flare of anger had died, and her face was expressionless. There was a coldness in her eyes which Charles found surprising, because he himself was moved. Almost for the first time since he had heard of the letters from Stacey, he found himself thinking of them not as a possible clue in a case of murder, not as treasure trove, and not even as historical documents of great interest, but as something far more personal, the product of the mind of a young man, at that time still quite obscure, but already carrying the burden of his genius, a young man whom Charles was proud to think of as his ancestor, but whose mind he had never troubled to understand. For that was not Charles's line, as it was Peggie's. The mere thought of trying to do such a thing would always scare him. But these letters, so nearly destroyed once before and saved only by some scruple of scientific piety in the limited mind of Frederick Robertson, would have brought the greatness of the earlier century close, made it human and at least partly comprehensible. And that that could never happen now

245

was something over which one might grieve for a lifetime.

Without touching it, Stacey was pointing at one of the scraps of paper.

"This one," he said, "has just three words on it. In the top line, the words, 'passionate attachment,' and immediately below them, 'phlogiston.' And I may say that in the juxtaposition of these words lies a problem which, I foresee, will delight and mystify scholars to all eternity. Phlogiston, as you are certainly aware, was thought at that time to be one of the components of air. So how did James Robertson come to be referring to two such apparently different concepts in what may well have been one sentence? Was the passionate attachment perhaps not to Franziska Münzinger, as one naturally at first assumes, but to science, truth or what-have-you? We shall never know. Never. So we may safely offer possible answers to the question according to the bias of our own temperaments. Personally I shall take the stand that since love is a very, very complex emotion, which might on occasion entwine itself even around phlogiston, he was referring to Franziska."

"And what's on the other one?" Charles asked.

"Ah, here's another fascinating mystery," Stacey said. "Again three words, though this time all on one line. '. . . my belief in . . .' And naturally we ask at once, belief in what? In God, in himself, in his theories?"

"I imagine," Peggie said thoughtfully, "you'll plump for his theories, won't you, Professor?"

"Why, that's remarkably shrewd of you, Dr. Robertson," he said. "Most likely I shall."

"After all, you've just had your theory about these letters vindicated," she said. "You know how important a theory can be to a man."

"Yes, that's true," he said. "That's very true."

"The letters existed," she said. "They were just where you worked out they ought to be. And that's making you pretty happy, even if all the rest have gone."

"It's at least some compensation for the terrible loss."

"For you."

"Yes, I'm afraid only for me. For you I can only express my deepest and sincerest sympathy. For you and all the others who would have found the letters of inestimable interest."

She had no patience with his sympathy. "Your reputation as a scholar is made now, isn't it?" she said. "In your own world, you'll be famous."

"Famous is a big word," he said.

"Why be afraid of a big word, when you haven't been afraid of much else?" she said.

He raised his eyebrows in a puzzled frown. Mrs. Stacey, whose big blue eyes were fixed in a stare of peculiar hardness on Peggie's face, leant towards him and whispered in his ear.

He gave his head a slight shake.

Peggie smiled. "I've an idea Mrs. Stacey and I understand one another," she said.

Stacey looked bewildered and incredulous. "If you're suggesting," he said hesitantly, "that there's some doubt of the authenticity of these fragments . . ."

"I'm suggesting," Peggie said, putting her fists on the table and leaning on them, bringing her face closer to his, "that there's doubt of every single thing you've told us. That there ever were any letters. That you ever believed there were. I'm suggesting that you forged those two small pieces of paper—a much easier thing to do than forging a whole pile of letters, and that you and your wife were in a conspiracy with the Baldreys to have them discovered just as they were. But something went wrong. Whichever of you was setting things up to look like a burglary got caught by my grandmother and killed her. And that was too much for David Baldrey, so he had to be killed too. And you did it as you did, and threw the rifle down where you did, because you meant to incriminate my cousin or me."

Charles had been trying to stop her. He had opened his mouth to speak several times. But at the same time he had been fascinated by her swift, quiet speech, and even when she had finished, he still said nothing.

Stacey seemed fascinated too, meeting her gaze helplessly and vacantly.

"Oh, Harlan!" his wife said. "Answer her, Harlan!"

George Nutting gave a high little giggle. Jean Baldrey swung round on him and said, "Be quiet!"

At last Stacey dropped his eyes, looking at the two small pieces of paper on the table as if he could not think what they were. Then he picked them up carefully, put them back in the envelope from which he had taken them and held out the envelope to Charles.

"It would be best, I think, if you would take charge of these, Mr. Robertson," he said. "You will, of course, have them examined by other experts. Tests can be made which will establish their age. Others besides myself are competent to give an opinion on whether the handwriting is or is not the handwriting of James Robertson. In the meantime we should, I believe, go to the Baldrey house to collect the ashes in the fireplace there. It is just possible that something may be learnt from a chemical analysis of them. The attempt is at least worth making, if Miss Baldrey will allow it."

"If you're going there, I'm coming too, to look after Miss Baldrey," Nutting cried, coming out from behind the bar and grabbing Jean by the arm. "Come on, Jean, we'll go in my car and we aren't letting them get there before us."

She started to resist, but as he thrust her towards the door, she changed her mind and hurried out of the room ahead of him. Charles and the Staceys followed, leaving Peggie, her self-assurance suddenly draining out of her, behind at the table. As they went she made a choked sound and covered her face in her hands. From the doorway of the White Lion, Charles saw Nutting and Jean get into a car that was next to the Staceys' in the small car park and drive off.

"Mr. Robertson, will you come with us?" Mrs. Stacey said. "If you'll tell me the way, I'll drive."

"Yes," Charles said. "Yes, I'll come."

But he did not move. As Nutting's car disappeared down the lane he had an extraordinary illusion. For Nutting was so short and his head so low above the wheel that he was invisible through the rear window, and if Charles had not known otherwise, he would have been ready to swear that the car was being driven by Jean, and that it had a left-hand drive.

# Chapter XIII

THE STACEYS were impatient. They were in their car already and asking Charles why he did not get in too. He had started towards them when Peggie came out of the doorway behind him. She looked dazed and only half aware of them all and was going to walk past them and go home when Charles took her by the arm and drew her towards the car.

He gave the Staceys a questioning look.

"Sure," Stacey muttered. "Get in, Dr. Robertson."

Peggie shook her head and said that she couldn't, yet she did not resist when Charles thrust her into the back seat and got in beside her. As Mrs. Stacey started the car, Peggie sank her head into her hands again, then raised it with a jerk and said, "I'm sorry—I'm very sorry. I had absolutely no right to make all those accusations. The evidence is altogether insufficient."

It was not really the most handsome of apologies, but Stacey said, "Forget it—I guess we're all under a strain."

She leant back and closed her eyes. Charles thought he had never seen her look so exhausted and forlorn, and his anger with her because she had broken her promise to him not to interfere and had created a situation of such embarrassment, subsided. He supposed that she must have been building far more than she had admitted on the hope that the letters existed and might be recovered and so had had to hit out at someone for what she had suffered when she learnt that they had been destroyed.

And the case that she had made out against the Staceys had been almost a good one. She had not explained why they should have used the Heydons' rifle for the murder of Baldrey, and her suggestion that they had chosen that risky and elaborate method of getting rid of him in order to cast suspicion on Charles or herself was not very convincing. But still there was plenty to think about in what she had said, just as there was plenty to think about in what Charles's solicitor friend had told him about the estate duty that might have had to be paid by anyone who had inherited the letters in the normal way.

That piece of information might become extremely important if Peggie were never able to prove that she had been to a cinema in London the evening before. Since seeing Nutting and Jean drive off together, Charles had realised that as usual he had been going much too fast when he had asserted that the car seen by Dainton must have been a foreign car. He had not stopped to think that there might be other explanations of that hand signal that Dainton had been able to see from his garden.

Mrs. Stacey was driving as slowly and carefully as she had said that she had driven

from Stratford. As they passed the Daintons' cottage, with the fresh pink curtains
at the windows and the new thatch that had
caught Charles's eye when he was on his
way to post his aunt's letter, he thought
that, as soon as he could, he would call there
to ask Dainton himself to tell him exactly
what he had seen. He did not see how it
could have been Jean, with Nutting driving,
in Nutting's car, if they had both still been
in the White Lion, clearing up in the bar.
And even if there was no one but themselves
to say that they had been there, what could
they have been doing, driving, not away
from the White Lion, but towards it, at ten
minutes past ten?

But these were the sort of questions,
Charles thought, to which only the police
would be able to find the answers, just as
only they could discover whether or not
Peggie had really been in London at the time
of Baldrey's murder, and Mrs. Stacey in
Stratford. There was really nothing that
Charles himself could do just then but bear
the questions in mind.

He had been giving Mrs. Stacey direc-
tions as she drove, and now they turned into
the farm drive. Nutting's car was in the yard
in front of the house. The door of the house

254

was open and Jean was in the doorway, waiting for them. She took them into the kitchen, where George Nutting was already stooping over the cold stove, peering inside it.

He whirled on them as they came in.

"Don't any of you touch anything!" he said. "This is for the police."

"Have the police been called?" Charles asked.

"No," Jean said. "George and I have been arguing. He didn't want me to let any of you in. I said I wanted Professor Stacey to see those ashes."

"I didn't want her to let you in," Nutting said, "because you've all got it in for her, Dr. Robertson saying she'd burnt the papers herself because she got frightened of hanging on to them, and then that she was in a conspiracy with the Staceys and everything, and nobody thinking of standing up for her. 'You'll find they're going to leave you holding the baby, the whole guilty crew,' I said. 'They're going to try and make out you killed your own brother,' I said, 'even though you've never fired a gun in your life, and poor Mrs. Robertson, too. They've had that arranged between them all along,' I said, 'or why did Mr. Robertson say he saw your brother in the car when it was you? If you'd listen to me——' "

"George—please!" Jean interrupted him fiercely. "I told you, Mr. Robertson said it was David because he thought it *was* David." She gave Charles a swift glance and with a pang he remembered that he had not yet apologised for his behaviour the evening before. "I'll call the police now," she went on. "Or perhaps——" She looked round the big kitchen uncertainly and Charles thought that although she did not want to admit it, she did not want to leave them all there unwatched in the same room as the ashes that might be so important.

"Would you like me to call them?" he suggested.

"Oh, will you?" she said. "The telephone's in the passage."

"Do you mind if I just look inside that stove first?"

"No—go on."

Stacey and Mrs. Stacey were already looking into the stove, with Nutting standing near them, his big hands clenched, as if he were ready to strike them down if they moved an inch closer to it.

Moving aside so that Charles could have his turn, Stacey said, "I don't know—I don't think there's much hope of finding anything out from that, but it's always worth trying."

Looking into the stove, Charles doubted if in this case it was. On the bars at the bottom there were a few grey cinders, and above them, on a ledge at the back, a small drift of flaky ash that just might once have been paper.

"Well, science is a wonderful thing if it can do anything with that," he said as he turned away and went to the door.

"Charles," Peggie said.

She had not gone to look into the stove, but as soon as she had come into the room, had dropped into a chair at the table and leant her hand on her hands.

"Yes?" Charles said from the doorway.

"Will you do something for me—if Miss Baldrey doesn't mind?"

"What is it?" he asked.

"Telephone Ivor for me. Tell him what's happened."

"Why not do it yourself?"

"In case Deborah answers." She spoke without any pretence that most of them in the room would not understand why she could not face speaking to Deborah.

Charles glanced at Jean, who nodded.

Going out into the passage, he closed the door of the kitchen behind him, and first rang up the police. He spoke to Inspector Long, telling him what he and his men had missed in their search of the farmhouse.

Long said sharply, *"Burnt?"* In a tone of self-disgust he added, "That's the one thing I never thought of."

A moment later Ivor almost exactly echoed him. "Burnt!"

Yet Long's exclamation had been a question, and Ivor's, Charles thought, was more like a confirmation of something that he had half expected to hear.

"You don't sound surprised," Charles said.

"Are you?" Ivor asked.

"Very surprised," Charles said. "Even more so that you aren't."

"Oh, in that case . . ." Ivor's loud laugh boomed suddenly in Charles's ear. It sounded a forced laugh, a noise he produced to give himself a little time to think, because he had made a blunder that had to be covered up. "After all, it's what people usually do with letters they steal, isn't it? They steal them on purpose to be able to destroy them, so that they can't be used against them—

unless, of course, it's the other way round, and they steal them to use for blackmail."

"Ivor, these letters were over two hundred years old. There can't have been anything in them that could have been used against anybody."

"Ah, you never know," Ivor said. "Letters are queer things. People put things into letters which later on they'd give their lives never to have written. Even next day, perhaps. Oh, lord, yes—the things one puts into letters!"

"James Robertson happens to have been dead rather a long time," Charles said. "I don't think he's worrying much."

"Still, you never know who else might be, do you? An indiscretion is always an indiscretion."

"That's where you're quite wrong. It takes far less than two hundred years to change it into a piece of harmless history."

Ivor's laugh roared out again, as unconvincingly as before.

"Don't let me give you the impression I'm that sort of a letterwriter myself," he said. "I never write to anyone except my agent. I can't bear the thought of putting pen to paper unless I know I'm going to be paid for it . . . What?" The last word had

259

not been spoken to Charles, but to someone, probably Deborah, who was in the room with him. "He said they were burnt—yes, burnt, burnt, burnt!" Ivor cried in a voice of rising frenzy.

"Ivor!" Charles said sharply. Then, as he heard another sound at his ear, he started to shiver, and quickly, as if the instrument in his hand had suddenly turned into something repulsive to touch, he slammed it down on its stand.

The sound had been Deborah's laughter, high, shrill, helpless.

Or so he had thought. Only an instant later, he found himself wondering if what he had heard had not been laughter but sobs. Probably he ought not to have rung off so soon. He ought to have tried to find out what the burning of the letters meant to Deborah. Yet when he thought of picking up the telephone again to interrupt whatever storm was now raging between the Heydons, he turned quickly and went back to the kitchen.

Peggie looked round at him. He said, "I told him." Then he went to the window and stood there, looking out, with his back to the room.

The window overlooked a tangled orchard in which primroses and daffodils bloomed in last year's unmown grass. The buds on the fruit-trees were swelling. The rain had stopped, but everything glistened with moisture. A hedge-sparrow, nest-building in mind, was hopping along a branch with a piece of straw trailing from its beak. Charles concentrated on the sparrow and for a moment found that it seemed to be really the only thing that mattered just then. And why shouldn't it be? Wasn't it generally considered an important matter if a sparrow fell to the ground?

The bird seemed to feel Charles's gaze upon it, dropped the straw and took flight. At the same moment, Charles heard the sound of a car in the drive and knowing that the police had arrived, he forgot the sparrow. Yet at a later time he found that whenever he thought of the final stages of the investigation, he had a clear picture in his mind's eye of the sparrow hopping along the branch of the apple-tree. By then he knew that it was as he had stood watching the bird and thinking over what Ivor had said to him, that he had first begun to understand the truth about the murders of Alice Robertson and David Baldrey.

Long and the sergeant came in together,

went to the stove and looked into it, then looked at the two fragments of the letters which Charles handed over to Long in the envelope in which they had been given to him by Stacey. The sergeant's neck and ears were red and his mouth was even more firmly closed than usual. Charles thought that he must have been responsible for the search that had failed to find any trace of the letters and that on the drive to the farm he had been listening to Long's opinion of him.

Long's phlegmatic face seemed less expressive than ever and had the slackness and greyness of a weariness that he had not shown before. One of his fingers, tapping the table, showed that tension had been mounting in him. The finger went on tapping while Jean told him how she had found the two charred pieces of paper, while Stacey explained the writing on them, while Mrs. Stacey explained her sudden arrival. Once or twice Long clenched his hand and made it hang at his side, but after a moment it was back on the table, with the finger tapping away.

Charles had turned back to the window and was staring out at the damp orchard, trying to recapture a thought about Ivor which a little while before had seemed immensely significant. But the voices distracted him, and as no one stopped him, he opened the back door and strolled outside.

Ivor, he thought, had expected to hear that the letters had been burnt. But he had not meant to give that away, and as soon as he had realised that he had done so, he had started to talk nonsense about the blackmail possibilities of letters two hundred years old. For the time being he had succeeded in creating a certain amount of confusion in Charles's mind, but now the tone in which Ivor had spoken that one word, "Burnt!" seemed more important than anything that he had said after it, except perhaps when he had shouted it again at Deborah.

"Burnt, burnt, burnt!" he had shouted, as if in derision at her stupidity, as if she too should have known without being told that the letters had been burnt.

"Mr. Robertson."

Charles had not heard anyone behind him, but when he turned he found Jean Baldrey standing not a yard away.

"Mr. Robertson, I want to apologise for what I said last night." she said.

"But that's my job," he said in surprise.

263

"Apologising, I mean. I'm sorry, truly sorry, for what *I* said last night."

"But you didn't say anything, you just walked out." She smiled. "If you thought some things you're worried about, you needn't apologise. I don't think anyone has to apologise for thoughts at a time like this."

"Then I didn't say . . . ? I didn't tell you . . . ?"

She shook her head.

With relief he remembered that his worst suspicions of her had burst upon him as he had strode away through the dark wood, and that in fact he had not said anything to her of his assumption that she and Ivor were in love with each other.

"But I said that horrible thing about David having talked to Mrs. Heydon, and Mrs. Heydon having probably talked to an old friend," Jean said. "Only I didn't mean it. It was just that you were so certain I was lying about the pink lipstick on the cigarette-ends in the car. I wasn't lying, so you made me angry, so I said what I did. But I never thought you'd killed David or Mrs. Robertson—well, not once I'd understood why you said you'd seen David in the car, when you'd really seen me. And I didn't think Mrs. Heydon had had anything to do with the murders either. I think she and David knew each other better than anyone realised, but that's all."

"You think your brother told her about the letters and she told someone else, don't you?" Charles said.

"I think that may have happened," Jean answered, "but I'm not sure about anything, except that I don't think she can have done the shooting herself, if she's short-sighted."

"Suppose she'd come a good deal closer than we've been thinking."

"Then the bus driver would have seen her."

"Do you know about the car that stopped by the pond just before the bus came along?" Charles asked.

She nodded. "The police told me about it this morning. Besides, I heard about it on the news. They want the driver to report to them. But they said it may have been a foreign car, so I don't see how it can have had anything to do with the case unless, of course, Mrs. Stacey wasn't really in Stratford on Avon."

"Suppose," Charles said thoughtfully, watching her carefully, "it wasn't a foreign car."

She shrugged her shoulders. "It was driven by a woman, they said. The only other woman mixed up in this is Dr. Robertson, and she's supposed to have been in London."

"Will you tell me some more about the cigarette-ends in the car," Charles said. "Are they still there?"

"I don't know. The police have got the car, so I don't know if they're still there or if they've taken them away. Taken them away, I should think."

"But in that case they were still in the car yesterday, until the police took the car."

"Well, I'm not really sure. I think they were. That ash-tray never got emptied until it was overflowing. David used to clean the whole car up wonderfully at very long intervals, but in between whiles he never touched it. So I expect those cigarette-ends were still there. I'd forgotten about them till last night. Why, does it matter?"

"Perhaps it doesn't."

"Only you think it does."

"I don't know what I think, except that I wish I could stop thinking. I wish I could remember the police probably know their job and leave it to them. I've a job of my own they don't interfere with. I ought to follow their example."

"I wish I had a job," Jean said.

"I thought you had," Charles said.

"Oh, not any more. I only stayed here because of David. I couldn't stay here now."

"What will you do?"

"Sell the farm first. It's so run down I don't suppose I'll get much for it, but it'll keep me going while I try to pick up where I left off."

"You mean you'll go back to the theatre."

"Yes. I wasn't too bad, you know. If I stick at it, I may get somewhere. But it's just sticking at it, whatever happens, that has a wonderful sort of attraction after living with David."

"I like your courage," Charles said.

She gave a shake of her head. "This isn't courage. Coming here took courage, but going back is easy." She turned her head at sounds from the kitchen, the slam of a door and then a loud voice, speaking excitedly. "That's Mr. Heydon," she said.

They went back into the house. Ivor was in the middle of the kitchen, facing Long across the big table. Peggie was standing close to him, all pretence gone and her love and her need of him naked in her face. But Ivor might not have known that she was in the room. No one mattered to him then but the man with the Plasticine face.

"Is it true that you found those letters here and that they'd been burnt?" he was shouting at Long. "Is it true? I've got to know for sure. *Is it true?*"

Long answered distantly, "Miss Baldrey found certain fragments which Professor Stacey has identified as having been written by James Robertson. There's also some ash with which our laboratories may be able to do something, though that's far from certain."

"Then you *aren't* sure! Those letters may still turn up somewhere else!"

"He *is* sure, Ivor," Peggie said. "We're all sure. They're gone, all but those two little pieces. We can stop hoping."

Ivor might not have heard her. She might not have existed. "How can you be sure they were all destroyed?" he shouted at Long. "Why should anyone destroy them?"

"I've told you the facts, Mr. Heydon," Long said. "You know as much as I do."

"But why should anyone destroy them?" Ivor repeated.

Long did not answer. Yet, as the two men

stared at each other, Charles had a feeling that in that moment of silence some argument that had been raging in Ivor's mind was brought to an end. He dropped his gaze, turned and went swiftly out of the room.

Peggie took a step after him, hesitated, then swayed. The silent sergeant caught her as she fell.

# Chapter XIV

SHE DID not quite faint. After a moment she was snapping that she did not want brandy, did not want anything but to be left alone. She sat limply on the same chair as before, leaning her head on her hand and looking vacantly into space.

Charles asked Long if his presence was necessary any more and Long shook his head, saying that he wanted some further discussion with Professor and Mrs. Stacey, particularly Mrs. Stacey. He would like, Long said, some details of how she had spent the evening before and the time at which she had received her husband's telephone call.

So Long had arrived, Charles realised, as earlier he had himself, at the point of believing that the car seen by Dainton was probably a foreign car. He had not, as Charles had since that time, seen Jean and George Nutting drive away together, and realised that what Dainton had seen might possibly be interpreted in a different fashion.

It was to the Dainton cottage that Charles now went, walking down the rough drive to the gate, then along the lane to the letter-box. When he reached the gate of the cottage, he saw a man working in the garden. He was a short wiry man with a peak of stiff white hair above a lively, weather-beaten face. In spite of his age, his movements as he stooped and straightened over a bed where he was pricking out some seedlings, were agile and precise. His eyes, as he looked up when he heard Charles's step on the path, were shrewd and bright.

"Good day," he said briskly. "What is it this time, detective, journalist, or just ordinary mortal, come to read a meter or to persuade me that the end of the world's at hand and it's time to repent? You don't look like one of those hawkers of doom. They all have a certain clear, cheerful, empty look in the eye that you can't mistake. And for reading meters you ought to be wearing a cap, or a badge or something. And your muscles aren't chunky enough for a detective. So I suppose you're a reporter. No, I've got it—insurance! You've come to sell me insurance."

Charles responded to his smile. "Actually you know who I am, don't you?" he said.

"Well, yes, Mr. Robertson, I do," Dainton said. He brushed some sticky soil from his hands. "Come inside and tell me what I can do for you. My wife and I knew Mrs. Robertson, you know. Not well, but she'd been a kind neighbour since we moved in here. We were both very grieved to hear of her death."

"I don't want to disturb you," Charles said. "I only came to ask a question."

"About the car I saw?"

"Yes."

"Well, come in, come in. I hope I can help. You know I can't tell you what sort of a car it was, don't you? I've never had any truck with the internal combustion engine. It isn't a question of principle, or anything like that—I try to get along without principles—it's just simple regard for public safety." He was leading Charles towards the cottage. "A bicycle is the farthest I've ever gone along the road of mechanisation of my own movements, and I gave that up years ago, when I found my front wheel always made contact with whatever solid object was in sight. It's some peculiar quirk of my mind, I suppose, because there's nothing wrong with my eyesight. Don't worry about that—my eyesight's all right. I know what I saw last night."

They had gone into the cottage through the front door that opened straight into a tiny sitting-room where an elderly woman with a mild, earnest face was at work at a sewing machine, making some frilly curtains. She fussed shyly over Charles, placing him in a chair, then made him change to another which might be more comfortable, insisted on making him some tea and scuttled away to do it through a little low doorway, like a rabbit into its burrow.

"Well now," her husband said when she had gone, "ask me what you like and I'll do my best to answer, but don't ask me if the car was a Ford or a Daimler or an Austin or a Morris, or if it was one or ten or twenty years old, because I don't know."

"Can't you tell me whether or not it was a big car?" Charles said.

"Big?"

"Yes, big. Very long, very wide."

"Those are all very relative words, aren't they?"

Charles saw that the old man was delighted with the position that he was in of important though unsatisfactory witness. Trying to keep his patience, Charles said, "Well, big in relation to almost every other car you've ever seen come down this lane."

"I'd have said myself it was just about average," Dainton said, "but perhaps it was big. No—no, I'll stick to average. An absolutely average car."

In that case, Charles thought, the Staceys' car could be ruled out without further questioning.

"I'd like you to tell me then," he said, "about the woman you saw in the car and the movement she made with her hand."

"Ah, that's much easier, I can tell one woman from another," Dainton said and chuckled raffishly. "Not that I'd recognise this one again. She had one of those scarf-things they wear tied under their chins which make them all look exactly alike. I should think those things are about the most democratising influence of our day, you know. From duchess to charwoman, they abolish all distinctions——"

"Yes," Charles said, "I agree. And what

it comes to is that you can't really tell me much more about the woman than the car —whether she was young or old, dark or fair, tall or short."

"Yes, I'm afraid that's true," Dainton said.

"And," Charles went on quickly, before Dainton could get started again, "you possibly can't be absolutely certain that she was alone in the car."

"Oh, come now, come now," Dainton said, "that's quite different. I know I saw only one woman, not two."

"She had no one sitting beside her?"

"Positively no one. And no one behind her either—unless, of course, there was someone hiding in the car. Is that what you're after? I suppose it's quite possible that someone was hiding behind the seat. I mean, if you've a reason for thinking that, I couldn't swear it wasn't so. From where I was standing in the garden I couldn't see down into the car, only straight through it, if you know what I mean."

"I see," Charles said. "Now can you tell me about this movement she made with her hand? Will you try to describe exactly what you saw?"

Dainton wrinkled his forehead, tugged

274

his chin and concentrated on a space in the air a little to the left of Charles's face.

"I was in the garden," he said. "I was going to meet the bus, but I was early. I went out early on purpose, to take a turn up and down the garden, as I often do late in the evening, to get a little fresh air before I go to bed. Like an old dog, eh, being turned loose before being shut up for the night? Well, there I was and this car came along and stopped at the bend by the pond."

"Was it coming fast or slow?" Charles asked.

"In my opinion, all cars go fast—very fast—much too fast."

"Yes. Well. Was this any faster than usual?"

Dainton gave this question careful thought. "Probably not—probably just about average," he said.

"And did it brake very suddenly at the corner, or just slow down and stop?"

"Aha," Dainton said, "I see what you're getting at. Did she see something happening down the lane that made her stop very suddenly, or did she just have some private sort of reason for stopping—wondering if she'd left her handbag behind, or something like that? Well, I think she stopped in a quite ordinary sort of way. She just got to the corner and stopped, as she might have if she'd wanted to get out. I can't remember anything sudden or dramatic about it."

"She didn't get out, did she?"

"Oh no. Positively, no. She just stuck her hand out and waved it a little, then pulled it in again and drove on."

"And on which side of the car did she stick her hand out?"

Dainton looked at Charles as if he thought him singularly stupid. "On this side of the car, of course, Mr. Robertson. I could hardly have seen what she did with her hand on the far side of it, could I?"

"I just wanted to be quite sure of that," Charles said. "What do you think she was doing when she waved her hand?"

"I thought she was making one of those traffic signals to show that she was stopping, or going to turn round, or something. I can't tell one from another, but I see drivers constantly doing it, for reasons that no doubt seem sufficient to them."

"Which side of the car was she sitting on when she made this signal?"

"Oh, the usual side, I think."

"Please, Mr. Dainton," Charles said, his voice suddenly rough and intense. "This is very important. It may even be the most important question you've ever been asked in your life. Which side of the car was the woman sitting on?"

Dainton's weathered cheeks reddened slightly. "I'm sorry, Mr. Robertson. I'm really trying to do my best. I said the usual side. I *meant* the usual side."

"Which do you think of as the usual side, the side nearer to your garden, or the side away from it?"

"The side away from it, of course."

"In that case, why did she make her signal on this side of her car?"

"I haven't the slightest idea. As I've tried to make you understand, I've never tried to penetrate the mind of the motorist, or to learn the conventions that govern his actions."

"You feel certain then that she wasn't in the seat on the near side of the car, and yet she put her hand out of the near window?"

"And what's wrong with that, I should like to know? She simply leant across and stuck her hand out."

"She *leant* across?"

"Of course."

"You saw that? You remember her leaning?"

"Well now, how on earth else could she have done it, unless her arms were about five feet long?"

"That's just what I wanted to know," Charles said. "Thank you, Mr. Dainton."

He stood up. All at once he was in such a hurry to leave that he forgot all about the tea that Mrs. Dainton was making. He mumbled his thanks over again as he made for the door, bumped his head violently against the low lintel of the door and stumbled out into the garden.

He heard exclamations of protest behind him but, rubbing the top of his head and blindly cursing, he strode away down the path, not knowing whether he was cursing at the pain of the bruise, at the shock of the knowledge that he now possessed, or at himself for having gone out to find it.

He walked away as fast as he could. Knowing that he was being watched from the garden by the two old people, he walked on past the pond and out of sight round the bend in the lane, and only then paused, and, after waiting for a minute or two, hoping that by then the Daintons might have gone back into the cottage to discuss his odd behaviour, went back to the pond.

It was a shallow, slimy expanse of water,

278

ringed with mud, rough grass and some discouraged clumps of reeds. Near the edge an old boot thrust its toe above the surface. The sole and the upper had parted from each other, and gaped like a fish's mouth above the water. A broken bottle, some rusted tin cans, some ice-cream wrappers and sodden cigarette packets lay in the mud. A smell of vegetable rottenness clung to the place.

Charles stepped over the low white railing at the edge of the road on to the narrow brink of mud beyond. He was not yet sure why he was there, whether it was to find proof of what he believed, or to make sure that no such proof existed. He did not know what he would do with it if he found it. He had loved Mrs. Robertson and had wished no ill to David Baldrey. That they had died as they had would fill his days and nights with horror for a long time to come. But he could envisage no relief for himself from that horror in thoughts of punishment, and there was almost as much pity in his mind for the murderer as for the two who were dead.

Perhaps that would change when he had had more time to think about it. Yet love can die hard, and he was gripped just then by a feeling of desperate protectiveness and of a fantastic loyalty which had never even been demanded of him. If at that moment he had seen one of the cigarettes that Deborah had smoked in Baldrey's car, and later thrown out of the car window, leaning across his dead body to empty the ash-tray, full of the incriminating stubs, into the pond, Charles might have set his foot upon it and pressed it deep into the mud.

But just as he caught sight of one of the small, flattened-out squares of pink-stained cork, caught in a tussock of grass, a car stopped beside the pond and Long got out. He came up to the railing and stood looking silently at Charles.

Cork, Charles was thinking. Her final disaster. If she had not smoked Baldrey's cigarettes with the cork tips, even the ones that had not fallen into the water would have disintegrated and disappeared in last night's rain. But at least one little piece of cork had survived, and was where Long, if he looked, as a moment later he did, could see it.

Long only glanced at it, as if he had known that it would be there, then looked back at Charles.

"Why must you go on trying to interfere, Mr. Robertson?" he asked in a voice which

Charles, bewildered, found not only quiet but oddly kind. "Why don't you leave it to us? This stage of things is bad enough even for us, and we're hardened, you know. Not perhaps as hardened as people sometimes think, but still none of you personally mean anything to us. We do a job and it goes in the records and we go on to the next one. But you'll have to live with this experience for the rest of your life. So why make it even harder for yourself than you need?"

Charles climbed back into the road. Mud clung to his shoes and he started trying to rub them clean on some grass at the side of the road. He seemed to be concentrating so hard on what he was doing that he might not have been thinking of anything else, but after a moment he asked, "Have you arrested her?"

"I haven't got to arrest her," Long said. "I haven't got to arrest anyone." He then added something under his breath about the sergeant, and Charles thought that he meant that the sergeant was making the arrest, but then, even in his dazed state, realised that Long was unlikely to be referring to the silent young man who dogged his footsteps as a fell sergeant, and that Long, almost as improbably had been quoting the line about

281

that fell sergeant, death, being strict in his arrest.

"Do you mean she's dead?" Charles asked.

"Yes," Long said. "Heydon telephoned the farm a few minutes ago. There was cyanide in the gardener's shed. She took it as soon as he left the house to go to the farm and find out if those letters had really been destroyed, as you'd told him. He'd suspected it from the first but had been clinging to the hope the letters would turn up somewhere. He knew she'd only have taken the letters to destroy them. She didn't want them, or the money they'd bring. She only wanted to prevent Dr. Robertson getting hold of them and being able to raise enough money for Heydon to be able to pension off his family. And the odd thing is, I don't believe he'd ever have left his wife, even if Dr. Robertson had got the money. But she wasn't to know that. Perhaps he didn't even know it himself. And perhaps I'm wrong. But it isn't usually money that decides these things."

"She didn't shoot Baldrey down the lane, did she?" Charles said. "She shot him at the farm."

"Yes, that's right. She wrote a short

confession before she killed herself. She shot him against the light he'd left on in the passage, because his sister didn't like coming home to a dark house. That was cunning, you know. Cunning and deliberate. If you're having trouble with your feelings about her, remember that. Your aunt's death was probably accidental. She says so in her letter. But unless you reckon that that accident drove her out of her mind, you've got to accept the fact that she set out coldly and carefully to murder Baldrey."

The difficulty that Charles was having with his feelings was that they seemed not to exist. He was unusually aware of a number of little things around him, as a short while ago he had been aware of the bird with the straw in its beak. A pebble on the road, a smear of cigarette ash on Long's raincoat, an insect darting above the pond, all seemed charged with mysterious importance, but inside he was cold and empty.

"I realised Heydon wasn't surprised about the letters having been burnt when I telephoned," he said. "He tried to cover it up with a lot of nonsense, but I noticed at the very beginning that he wasn't surprised. But I still don't know why. I don't know why he suspected her."

"Perhaps it was a natural thing to do if you really knew her," Long said. "And he saw her, remember, only a little while after each murder. While we were worrying about whether or not we could believe in the alibi she'd given him, he may have realised that he couldn't really give her one, and perhaps because she'd obviously been running, or was abnormally excited, he started to worry about what she'd been doing. He may even have been pretty sure it was she who removed the gun, though he did his best to cover up for her. What I'd like to know, though, is what started you on her track, Mr. Robertson. You must have been a long way ahead of me."

"Well, for one thing, I knew I hadn't heard any shot," Charles said. "You didn't have to believe me about that, but I was sure."

"And what else?"

"When I heard about the car Dainton had seen, I worked out it must have been a foreign car and I told her so. She'd had hysterics when she first heard about the car having been seen, and when I told her about its being foreign she was wild with relief. She kept saying it couldn't have anything to do with the case. I thought that was because she'd been afraid the driver of the car had been someone who'd been there at a time prearranged with Heydon, so that he could shoot Baldrey then, and afterwards point out, as he did, that Baldrey could only have been shot when the bus came along. But later, when I realised the car hadn't necessarily been a foreign one, I thought it could have been the sheer terror of discovering that she'd been seen that gave her the hysterics."

Long nodded. "How did you work out that she'd killed Baldrey at the farm?"

"I worked backwards to it," Charles said, "from thinking that what Dainton might really have seen was someone leaning over from the driver's seat of the car and throwing something into the pond. Jean Baldrey had told me she thought her brother and Mrs. Heydon knew each other better than people thought, because she'd seen some cigarette-ends in the car, marked with the colour Mrs. Heydon wore, and Baldrey got angry when she asked him about them. But you didn't seem to be asking any questions about them, so I thought they couldn't be in the car any longer. And who would have troubled to get rid of them but Mrs. Heydon herself? And if it was she whom Dainton had seen doing that, then she was coming away from the farm in the Baldreys' car. In that case, when did Baldrey get into the car, unless he was in it with her, doubled up dead in the passenger's seat? If she'd stood at the end of the path through the wood, where it joins the farm drive, she could have shot him against the light in the house just after he'd got into the car. She wasn't a good shot, but at that range she could have managed it. And he had to be killed in the car itself, because he'd have been too heavy for her to lift into it. Then she could have run into the house, pushed the letters into the stove, and the hollowed-out volume of the Proceedings into the dustbin. She'd have known the book would be found and thought it would fasten suspicion for the theft on Baldrey, but that it would never be known what he'd done with the letters. Then she could have pushed his body across into the other seat, driven to the usual place, pushed him back into the driver's seat and got home before the bus went by, so that her husband would give her an alibi for that time. And it made sense of the rifle having been left where we found it. She wanted to do everything to make us think that Baldrey had been shot from that end of the lane, at a range that would have been beyond her."

"She took a good many risks, didn't she?"

"I don't think she'd much choice. I think Baldrey had forced her hand, telling her he was going to you. And I think she may have persuaded him to wait, saying she'd come over to the farm in the evening and explain, or something like that. I went over there to try to see him myself a bit earlier in the evening and I'm sure he was in, but he wouldn't answer the door. I didn't understand it at the time, but if he was watching for her and didn't want me around when she came, it makes sense."

"There was quite a risk the children would wake up and find she was gone, wasn't there? If they'd talked about that later, it would have spoilt everything."

"When I was over there later in the evening, Heydon remarked on how soundly they were sleeping. Don't you think she'd given them each one of his sleeping pills?"

"You seem to have thought of everything, Mr. Robertson. Of course I've kept hearing for the last couple of days that you come of an unusual family, yet I underrated you, which was stupid."

"Where are the children now?" Charles asked.

"They're at your house. Heydon's not in any state to look after them, and Dr. Robertson can only think about Heydon. I'll bet you anything, though, that those two will never marry. They'll put it off for a while now for decency's sake, then, all of a sudden, Heydon will go and marry another adoring, possessive woman and settle down again to being unfaithful to her and worrying himself sick about her. And somewhere at the back of her mind, Dr. Robertson will be rather relieved and will settle down to science and turn up at the top one day."

This was the man, Charles thought, whom Ivor had carelessly written off as stupid, mainly because he hadn't liked his face.

"You're saying pretty much what Miss Baldrey said about her brother," Charles said. "She didn't believe he'd really change."

"He wouldn't have, either. She's lucky to get free. She's all broken up now, but in a day or two she'll be telephoning theatrical agents and packing to leave for London. And the Staceys will be leaving too. They were fighting it out when I left the farm whether the next port of call was to be Stonehenge or Edinburgh. You'd think, after the last few days, that even Professor Stacey would have had enough of the Robertsons, but it seems he's still got to see the place where your ancestor was born."

"Who's looking after the children?" Charles asked. "Is Mrs. Harkness still there? I thought she usually went home before this."

"No, she isn't there," Long said. "I left the pair of them in the care of the Scottish lady. She seemed a reliable type and she seems to understand children. She started straight away teaching them how to hit a golf-ball, which is probably as good a way as you'd find of keeping their minds off what's been happening around them."

"For God's sake!" Charles shouted. "Why didn't you tell me she was here? When did she come? How did she get here?"

"She said she heard something about the murders on the radio and came straight down by plane."

"And I've been standing here . . . !"

Charles was not standing there any longer when he said that. He was already some way off down the lane.

He had been telling himself over and over again that day that there was no point in telephoning Sarah again. Because it was Sunday, she could not have received his letter yet, and was almost certain, he had been convinced, to be away somewhere, playing golf. He had felt angry with her all day, had almost hated her, because of that conviction of his. And all the time, she had been on her way here. Golf clubs and all, she had come when he needed her.